PENGUIN BOOKS

DOLLAR BAHU

Born on 19 August 1950 in Shiggaon, north Karnataka, Sudha Murty is a renowned author, philanthropist, teacher, engineer, visionary and leader. As founder of the Murty Trust, she is dedicated to preserving and celebrating art, cultural heritage, science and research, Indian books and manuscripts, and knowledge systems born in India. Murty's literary works have captured readers' hearts with their simplicity, warmth and insight. From novels and short stories to travelogues, her books have been translated into all major Indian languages, selling over 30 lakh copies around the country. Several of her books have also been translated into Italian and Arabic. Among her most famous titles are *Grandma's Bag of Stories*, *Gently Falls the Bakula*, *Three Thousand Stitches* and *Wise and Otherwise*. Her writings are informed by values of compassion and kindness, in keeping with our culture and heritage. Her non-fiction stories are based on her time at the Infosys Foundation, where she worked with people from all walks of life.

Through the Infosys Foundation, Murty established numerous schools, hospitals and orphanages across India, impacting the lives of thousands of individuals. Over the years, her efforts have been recognized with many honorary doctorates and prestigious awards, including the Padma Bhushan and the Padma Shri from the Government of India in 2023 and 2006, respectively; the R.K. Narayan Award for Literature in 2006; and the Lal Bahadur Shastri National Award in 2020. She was also awarded the Rajyothsava and the Dana Chintamani Attimabbe Award for excellence in Kannada literature by the Government of Karnataka in 2000 and 2012, respectively.

SUDHA MURTY

dollar bahu

PENGUIN BOOKS

An imprint of Penguin Random House

PENGUIN BOOKS

USA | Canada | UK | Ireland | Australia
New Zealand | India | South Africa | China | Singapore

Penguin Books is part of the Penguin Random House group of companies
whose addresses can be found at global.penguinrandomhouse.com

Published by Penguin Random House India Pvt. Ltd
4th Floor, Capital Tower 1, MG Road,
Gurugram 122 002, Haryana, India

First published by Eastest Book (Madras) Pvt. Ltd 2005
Published by Penguin Books India 2007
This edition published in Penguin Books by Penguin Random House India 2023

Copyright © Sudha Murty 2006, 2007

63 62 61

ISBN 9780143103769

This is a work of fiction. Names, characters, places and incidents are either the
product of the author's imagination or are used fictitiously and any resemblance
to any actual person, living or dead, events or locales is entirely coincidental.

Typeset in Sabon by S.R. Enterprises, New Delhi
Printed at Thomson Press India Ltd, New Delhi

www.penguin.co.in

TO MY SISTER JAISHREE

PREFACE

It gives me immense pleasure that my book *Dollar Bahu* is being published by Penguin. The original book, *Dollar Sose*, written in Kannada, has been translated into Marathi, Telugu, Tamil, Hindi, Malayalam and Gujarati, and has also been prescribed as a textbook for undergraduate students in some Karnataka universities.

This story can happen in any part of India but I have set it in Karnataka, the region most familiar to me. I hope the book will show some families that love and affection can be more important than money.

Sudha Murty

With growing impatience, Chandra Shekhar stood on the platform, waiting for the Rani Kittur Chennamma Express. The train left Bangalore in the night, went via Hubli and Dharwad, and terminated at Kolhapur in Maharashtra. The rake had not yet arrived on the platform. He had come to the station too early. His younger brother Girish, who had come to see him off, had gone off with a hurried, 'I'll get you some magazines, be back in a couple of minutes', half an hour ago, and was nowhere to be seen.

That was Girish, easily distracted, fickle, almost irresponsible. He had probably met some friends and lost track of time. Chandru on his part was a sharp contrast to Girish—punctual, organized, thorough, systematic and ahead of time in everything. Chandru kept glancing at his watch. Finally he saw the train approaching the platform. He relaxed a bit, but something was bothering him. Born and bred in Bangalore, he had hardly even been to nearby Mandya or Mysore, and certainly never to this place, Dharwad. To him it was only a spot on the map of Karnataka.

Had he been a computer engineer, he would not have had to leave Bangalore. In fact people from all over India came to Bangalore for software jobs. But he was a civil engineer with a very reputed company in Bangalore and now, because of his efficiency at work, he had been specially selected to supervise a project in north Karnataka.

He had accepted this transfer rather reluctantly. On his way to take up his duties in an unknown place, among unknown people, he felt like a newly-wed bride leaving her beloved parental home with mixed feelings of joy and apprehension.

Just as the train pulled in, Girish appeared from nowhere. He picked up the luggage and said, 'Don't worry, Chandru, I'll put the luggage inside. You take your time.'

Deep in thought, Chandru followed his brother into the compartment.

'Okay, Chandru, goodbye. Telephone us when you reach,' said Girish, and jumped off. Chandru looked around at his co-passengers cursorily, and then turned his attention to the magazine Girish had bought for him. Soon the train began to move. Chandru looked out of the window at waving hands and people shouting goodbye and final pieces of advice. He had no one to wave out to. Girish was long gone. With a sigh, Chandru stared out of the window. He was travelling by train after a long time, and was not familiar with the sights along the railway track. It was quite interesting to identify the areas the train was passing through. He realized that his co-passengers were busy in their own conversations.

Chandru did not understand some of the expressions they used because, though the same language, the Kannada spoken in Dharwad has a very different accent and intonation. Perhaps because Dharwad is five hundred kilometres to the north of Bangalore and had been, for ages, part of the erstwhile Bombay Presidency. But Chandru understood the gist of their conversation. They were talking about music and the weather. Naturally. Because Dharwad was an important centre of Hindustani classical music.

Suddenly, an old man sitting next to him asked in a friendly and familiar manner, 'Where are you going?'

Sudha Murty

'Dharwad.'

'To whose house? Are you going on duty? Are you travelling alone?'

Chandru was taken aback by the flurry of questions. Being a rather shy and introverted person, he answered briefly, 'I will be there for a few months,' and left it at that.

When his office had instructed Chandru to leave for Dharwad within a week's time, Chandru had been extremely upset. He was quite happy where he was, and did not look forward to any disruption in the routine of his life. Seeing his long face and his reluctance to go, Girish had tried to cheer him up. 'What's the matter with you, Chandru? It's only another part of our own state, and you will be away for just a few months. Look at our Kitty. He too was reluctant when he was sent there on deputation for a year, but now he has settled there for life! He has become a typical Dharwad-kar, doesn't even bother to visit Bangalore during holidays.' Krishna Murthy was a good friend of Girish's. He was an officer in a bank and had promised Girish that he would take care of Chandru and make his stay comfortable. 'Chandru can stay with me as long as he likes,' he had said, adding, 'and my mother, a great cook, will be happy too have him. She has also picked up some local dishes, so Chandru can enjoy both varieties of food.'

In spite of these repeated reassurances, Chandru was determined not to spend more than a couple of days with Kitty. His thoughts were interrupted by the old man. Unfazed by Chandru's abrupt answer earlier, he said most cordially, 'Come, join us for dinner.' As politely as he could, Chandru refused, but that didn't deter the old man. He kept starting up a conversation on one pretext or another.

As Chandru stared out of the window, marvelling at the hospitality of the old man, he heard a beautiful voice from the adjoining compartment.

In the lush green forest, the koel proves to sing
Shunning in contempt all the powers of the king.

It was indeed a sweet voice and captivated Chandru completely. Even the other passengers, engaged in having their dinner, were immersed in the magic of the unseen singer's voice.

When the song ended, he heard a round of applause. 'Once more Vinu, please,' he heard some young voices clamouring for an encore. So, the girl with the golden voice was called Vinu, short for Vanita or Vineeta, he thought. He wanted to get a glimpse of her, but inhibition held him back.

'Vinu, we knew that you would bag the first prize in the competition. The judge was nodding his head in appreciation while you were singing.'

'Maybe, but that won't make me sing another song now. We reach Dharwad early in the morning. If we over-sleep then we may land up at Londa. All right, in the college ladies' room tomorrow I will sing for you. Go to sleep now,' Vinu scolded her companions gently.

Chandru concluded that these young college girls had taken part in a music competition in Bangalore and were now on their way back home. The thought that they were getting off at Dharwad cheered Chandru up somewhat.

'Excuse me, this is my berth. Can you please vacate it? I want to sleep.'

Chandru recognized the voice instantly. Vinu. He turned to look at her. She was fair with bold and beautiful black eyes, a straight, sharp nose, and long, thick hair braided into a plait. She seemed slightly flustered to find someone occupying her seat.

Chandru stared at her shamelessly. She was wearing a simple cotton Ilkal sari and no jewellery. He had not expected the girl with the golden voice to also be such a beauty.

'Could you please get up? This is my berth.' She sounded a little impatient.

This brought him back to reality. 'No, no, it is my seat. You are making a mistake.'

He showed her his ticket which said G-28.

'But see, my ticket is also G-28,' Vinu countered.

Chandru read the ticket: Vinuta Desai, F, 19, G-28. Obviously both of them had been allotted the same berth.

From the name on the ticket Chandru learnt that Vinu stood for Vinuta.

The clerk who was responsible for this confusion was probably sleeping soundly in Bangalore, leaving these two young people to sort it out. Chandru went to the ticket examiner, who dismissed it as an oversight and promised them that he would arrange for another berth at the next station. He requested them to manage till then.

Quite courteously Chandru told Vinu, 'You take this berth. I will wait till the next station.'

'Thank you. I am sorry for the trouble,' Vinu said softly.

'No trouble at all.'

Vinu settled down in her berth while Chandru went and stood near the door, waiting for the next station. The cold breeze sweeping his face heightened the unexpected pleasure he had experienced when he had encountered the golden-voiced beauty.

Chandru was quite unprepared when the train pulled into Dharwad station the next morning. He hurriedly jumped out from his compartment, still in his lungi. When he realized that he had not changed, Chandru was most embarrassed. A lungi on a railway platform! For heaven's sake, what had come over him!

Dharwad station reminded him of Mysore—small, neat and quiet. Chandru looked about for his charming co-passenger but she was nowhere to be seen. He felt disappointed.

Suddenly he heard a booming voice. 'Hey Chandru! Did you come by train or walk? You are the last passenger to get off. Looks like you overslept. Thank god you woke up in time, or else you would have had to see Belgaum, Miraj and Kolhapur.' It was Girish's friend, Kitty. Asking all the questions and answering them himself.

'Oh, hello. Just give me five minutes, I will change.' Chandru went to the waiting room, ignoring Kitty's questions and his replies.

Kitty picked up Chandru's suitcase and the two of them walked out. There were plenty of rickshaws and a few horse-drawn tongas waiting for customers.

'Can we take a horse-cart?' Chandru asked enthusiastically, like a child.

'Dharwad is a city of seven hills, like Rome, and seven lakes. If we take a tonga, we will have to get down and walk when we have to go uphill. Let's take a rickshaw today. We will reach home faster.'

Kitty's mother welcomed Chandru warmly. 'How are you, Chandru? How is your mother? How is Girish? How was the journey?'

'Aunty, all are fine. My journey was great,' replied Chandru, thinking of Vinu with the golden voice and enchanting face.

'You can stay with us as long as you need to, Chandru. No need for any inhibitions.'

'That is very nice of you,' he said, and then turning to Kitty, added, 'but please find me a room as quickly as possible. I would not like to impose on you for very long.'

∽

After breakfast, Kitty took Chandru around town on his bike and showed him the university campus, the famous peda shop and some lush parks.

It was the month of Shravan, the rainy season. All of Dharwad was celebrating, the city a riot of colour. Against the rich red earth, the trees, shrubs and bushes displayed every shade of green. The air was fragrant with the scent of flowers, bright yellow champak, creamy white rajnigandha, flaming orange marigold, delicate white jasmine and roses in all shades of red and pink. It was quite romantic, the atmosphere. 'Our Dharwad is like heaven,' said Kitty.

Chandru agreed with him, but in his mind he was thinking, Dharwad is a sweet enchanting girl while Bangalore is a ravishing woman. And while he could appreciate innocence, he was definitely more attracted to glamour.

∽

After a couple of days, Kitty told Chandru, 'There is a place available for a paying guest. If you are interested, we can go and see it.'

Chandru went with Kitty to see the place.

It was located in Malamaddi, one of the seven hills that Kitty had talked about earlier. After they came up a rough and rather steep road, they saw a house. In the middle of a spacious plot, enclosed by a fence, sprawled an old red-tile-roofed bungalow, surrounded by a vast lush garden. Chandru noticed mango, jackfruit and banana trees growing on one side. Closer to the house were beds of multicoloured flowers, and bushes of fragrant jasmine. He was surprised to see a tall parijata tree and the rare bakula with its dainty brown flowers next to it. Several varieties of champak dotted the rest of the garden. It was a charming spot, without a doubt. Chandru had not seen such a pretty house in Bangalore, especially in his locality, where most of the houses were three-storeyed buildings occupying the entire plot. Home gardens in such areas meant little plants grown in small pots.

Kitty knocked on the door and waited. Chandru couldn't believe his eyes. The person who opened the door was Vinu!

Oblivious to Chandru's open-mouthed look, Kitty asked her, 'Is this Bheemanna's house?'

Vinu was equally surprised. But she quickly gathered her wits about her and replied, 'Yes. Please come in. I will call my uncle.'

Chandru looked around the drawing room. The furniture was old and shabby, the walls unpainted. Obviously the family had seen better days.

Bheemanna, a man with a loud voice and a jolly manner, came out to meet them. Kitty introduced Chandru and explained the purpose of their visit. Enthusiastically, Bheemanna showed them an upstairs room. Chandru had already made up his mind. Whatever the rent, he would agree to it.

On the way home, Kitty remarked in a slightly impatient voice, 'You should have seen a couple of more places. The rent is a little steep. You should have at least said you will think it over.'

Chandru replied with a smile, '*Pehla pyar, pehla nasha.*' And walked away, leaving Kitty completely puzzled.

There was nothing special about the sunrise that morning, but when Vinuta stepped out of the house with a broom and a bucket to clean the garden, she felt it was a spectacular sight. The sun was dazzling in the bright blue sky, the air alive with the chirping of birds and the bakula and parijata flowers gave off a heady scent. Together, it was quite an intoxicating feeling, thought Vinu. The radiance of the morning was reflected in her face and echoed in the joy she felt in her heart. Vinuta gathered the bakula flowers that had fallen to the ground and, smelling their gentle fragrance, closed her eyes in a moment of happiness. Chandru watched her from the window upstairs.

Tring . . . tring . . . The milkman's cycle bell at the gate brought Vinu out of her reverie, reminding her to collect the milk and hurry up with the day's chores.

৵

Bheemanna Desai, Chandru's large-hearted and friendly landlord, had told him on the very first day, 'Don't consider yourself as just a paying guest. Look upon this as your own house.'

Within a few days Chandru had figured out that it was a big joint family, but he had not worked out the relationships between the members. One thing that had struck him in this short time was that the major share of the housework was done by Vinu. Even from his room on the terrace, he could hear someone or the other calling out for her, 'Vinu, have you plucked the flowers for puja?', 'Vinu, where are the ironed clothes?', 'Vinu, where is the bigger kadai?', 'Vinu, add some salt to the dal', and so on. Who was she really? A maidservant, an orphan, a poor relation, a housekeeper or . . .? But then she addressed Bheemanna Desai as uncle and he knew she went to college. . . It was a mystery to Chandru.

Then, one day, while talking to Bheemanna, he realized the house belonged to Vinuta, who had inherited it from her parents. They had died when she was very young, and Bheemanna, a distant uncle, had moved in here with his family to take care of her. This dilapidated house was the only thing she owned.

On Saturdays, his weekly holiday, Chandru preferred to stay at home and relax rather than go out in the hot sun along the dusty roads. On one such Saturday, he was woken up from a deep sleep by Vinuta's dulcet voice, singing as she watered the plants.

'Do you have to keep singing all the time? Do some worthwhile work at least some time. If you sit in the garden the whole day, who will do the housework? The dirty vessels are piling up. I am sick of reminding you about every task. God knows when your madness for music will go away.' A croaky voice interrupted Vinuta's song. Abruptly she stopped singing and ran inside.

Without realizing it, Chandru compared Vinuta with his sister Surabhi. Though she could sing reasonably well, Surabhi had neither the interest nor the dedication for music and though Chandru had often tried to persuade her to take music seriously, she would refuse under some pretext or the other. Whereas, Vinuta had a golden voice and deep dedication, but no opportunity to pursue it! Despite all the scolding and the heavy housework, she would hum happily to herself, and carry on. It upset Chandru much more than it did Vinuta. It was not long before the talkative Bheemanna passed on most of the family's history and background to Chandru. Seetakka, the elderly lady, was Bheemanna's mother. Bheemanna himself had four children. Vinuta was his niece. Bheemanna had only a modest income and had to try hard to make both ends meet, but he was a generous man and always a good host to the stream of guests who walked in throughout the day.

Bheemanna was very fond of Vinuta and wanted her to complete her degree, work for two years in order to become financially independent and then marry. At present she was in the second year of the BA degree course in Karnatak College, majoring in Hindustani music. A bright and talented girl, she had won almost every prize in every event in the college.

Every night, after dinner, Bheemanna would sit on the bamboo cot underneath the mango tree and relax for some time. That was the time when he also talked to Vinuta. 'Vinu, come here. You have done enough work for the day. Let the others also do something. What did you learn in the college today? Come on. Sing me a nice song now.'

When Chandru heard that, he would immediately come to the window and listen.

The sun was shining brightly on that day when Vinuta walked on to the terrace with a big cane basket full of ripe tamarind pods which she was going to spread out to dry. Knocking on Chandru's room door she asked timidly, 'Do you mind if I spread the tamarind in front of your room?'

She was speaking to him for the first time since he had moved in.

Chandru smiled. 'Of course you can. The tamarind and the terrace are both yours,' he said.

He knew she would go away soon after her work was done, but he hoped she would linger on.

'You sing so beautifully,' he complimented her, eager to strike a conversation.

'Thank you,' Vinuta responded shyly.

'Why don't you sing on the radio?'

'I do, I have been, for the last four years.'

Chandru felt rather stupid. 'Sorry, I did not know that. Please tell me when your next programme is going to be aired, I will definitely listen.'

'I will. But now, will you please step aside so that I can go?' Chandru drew back, abashed, and Vinuta left with a smile.

∽

As the days passed, Chandru became more familiar with Dharwad city and its surroundings, as also with the Desai family.

Sometimes, Bheemanna would invite him to join them for dinner. Vinuta rarely spoke much but her friendly smile warmed his heart.

Chandru went to play a friendly cricket match with his team . . . and returned with a dislocated elbow. The doctor put him in a plaster for three weeks and advised him rest for a week. Before he could think of going to Bangalore to recover, Bheemanna came to him and made an offer. 'Don't go to Bangalore. We will take care of you. Vinuta is here and she will serve you all your meals in your room.'

Without waiting for Chandru's response, he called out to Vinuta and said, 'Vinu, now you are in charge of Chandra Shekhar, until he is up and about. Don't give him the hard rotis that we eat. Prepare rice for him. Serve him coffee, not tea . . .'

Bheemanna wasn't just being formal; his warm heart genuinely wanted to be of help. Chandru felt this was an additional responsibility for Vinuta. He felt sorry for the poor girl. Of course, he had never seen her unhappy, tearful or angry. Perhaps, he thought, she shed her tears while watering the garden and no one in the house knew of her sadness. Only when she got married and went away would they realize the value of her presence, thought Chandru bitterly.

Just then Vinuta came with a cup of piping hot coffee. And her beautiful shy smile. Chandru could find nothing to say.

✧

One afternoon Chandru heard the excited chatter and uninhibited giggles of the young girls of the family sitting under the jackfruit tree and discussing saris for Diwali.

'Good thing Kaka has gone to Bangalore for some work, we could give him our specific requests for saris. I have asked for an aquamarine sari with a pink border,' said Vinuta, excitedly. Chandru was pleased to hear Vinu sounding so happy.

The following night, after dinner, he heard Bheemanna telling Vinu, 'Vinu, I could not get the exact colour you had asked for. Instead I have got this for you.'

'Oh, that's all right. This is also very pretty. I like this blue colour,' said Vinu brightly.

Vinuta's answer came as a surprise to Chandru. So unlike his sister Surabhi's reaction, he thought. Surabhi was the same age as Vinuta. The last time he had gone to Bangalore, he had had to trudge after her through all the shops in Chickpet just because she had wanted a particular 'shocking pink' sari. When she had been unable to find it, had she settled for the next best? Not a chance. She had dragged him to the market again the next day and finally bought a sari at twice the price he had budgeted for. Chandru had wanted to tell her that it looked awful on her dusky skin, but the thought of the possible consequences had made him keep his counsel. Vinuta, by contrast, seemed to be well aware of circumstances and adjusted to every situation. Of course, Surabhi's case was different. She had doting brothers and parents who were ready to spend time and money on her. She could afford to be choosy and insistent.

Chandru thought he was the only one who sensed and understood the hidden pain and helplessness behind Vinuta's captivating smile. The next day he asked Vinuta, 'How would you describe the colour aquamarine? Is it closer to blue?'

'It is blue mixed with a little green. But why do you ask?'

'Just curious, that's all,' he replied. It would have been very easy for him to buy a sari for someone who had taken such good care of him during his illness. But he was not sure how the gesture would be interpreted by the rest of the family, so he dropped the idea. As it is, Chandru's behaviour and close involvement with the Desai household had caused Kitty to tease him one day. 'Chandru, what's cooking? You hardly ever visit us. All the time you are stuck at Desai's house.'

'Absolutely nothing,' Chandru had retorted sharply. 'I have begun to like Dharwad, the way you have.'

'Is it Dharwad or the koel in Desai's house?'

'What do you mean?' asked Chandru.

'Well, most eligible bachelors have an eye on her.'

'What about you?'

'Oh no, my marriage has been fixed with a Bangalore girl. Are you . . .?'

'No. Unless I settle down to my satisfaction, there is no question of marriage.'

Suddenly, one day Chandru got instructions from his head office to report back to Bangalore immediately since he was being sent to America on deputation within a month's time. Chandru was overjoyed. America, to him, was the promised land, the land of milk and honey.

He had wanted to go there for higher studies but financial constraints at home had not allowed it. Then he had hoped to study computer science so that he could get a job abroad. Unfortunately, his average performance in the engineering entrance exam only got him a seat in the civil engineering department. His spirits hit rock bottom because it was the end of his American dream. But now, ironically, it was his civil engineering qualifications and his performance at work that had brought him the opportunity to go to the land he had been dreaming of for so long.

He came home that evening and immediately told Bheemanna that he would be leaving. He explained the reason. Bheemanna, too, was happy that the young man whom he had come to like was going abroad. 'Congratulations Chandra Shekhar Rao. You are going abroad. You must visit Dharwad sometime and stay with us.'

'Certainly. And whenever you come to Bangalore, you must come to our house,' Chandru extended a cordial invitation in return.

'Yes. My sister Indu stays in Rajajinagar. She has called me over quite a few times. I will make a trip to Bangalore sometime.'

Chandru went to the market to buy Dharwad pedas and then, thinking of Vinuta, he bought a book of poems.

As he was leaving for the station, he gave Vinuta the book. 'I am sorry I couldn't hear you on the radio. I don't get Dharwad radio station from Bangalore or anywhere else. Good luck.'

Chandru looked at Vinuta and felt a sadness emanating from her. She would probably miss him. Though they did not talk to each other a lot, she knew he was a music lover and her ardent fan.

She on her part felt this was probably their last meeting. Why would he come back to Dharwad or why would she go to Bangalore? Even if she did, what excuse would she have to meet him?

Shamanna, a Sanskrit teacher, was a calm, sensible and contented man. He had a reputation as a good teacher and a good human being. Gouramma, his wife, was a clever woman who knew how to run the family. She worked hard to keep the domestic expenses within the budget, but she was extremely ambitious. She always dreamed of diamonds, gold and silver jewellery, cars, a big house, servants . . .

Shamanna had a modest salary but he had managed to build a small house in Jayanagar. His priorities were different from his wife's. He wanted his children, Chandra Shekhar, Girish and Surabhi, to have a good education. So he did not think of extending his house or making any changes. Since her husband had been unable to fulfil her dreams, Gouramma had pinned her hopes on her children. Whenever she attended a marriage or a family function, she would look at the women wearing expensive silk saris and diamond earrings with envy and tell herself that they were so lucky.

In most such gatherings, it was customary for women who had travelled abroad to form an exclusive circle. Most of their children were settled abroad, so their conversation was usually different from that of the others. 'Oh, when I was in New York the last time, I bought a coral set,' one would say and another would remark, 'But you know jade is available only in San Francisco. I bought a beautiful jade set there.' A third would say, 'In Florida, you get the best quality green cardamom and Spanish saffron. I only use that to make sweets like kesari and all.' And poor Gouramma would feel completely left out. She felt people ignored her and looked down upon her because none of her children were based abroad. Every day she would pray to god that her children should go abroad and earn lots of money so that she could join that circle and tell them, 'See, I am equal to you.'

Chandru was Gouramma's favourite child. Like her, he was fair-complexioned, slightly built, with a pleasant, intelligent face. He shared her dream of going abroad. Girish, on the other hand, was tall and dark-complexioned, having taken after his father. A commerce graduate, Girish worked as a clerk in a bank. He was contented and happy with his lot. After office he would involve himself in all sorts of cultural activities such as compering programmes during the Dusherra festival, Ganesha Chaturthi, and Kannada Rajyotsava. If anyone required help at the bank, Girish would be the first to offer and muster help, be it a medical emergency, a funeral, or celebrations for a happy occasion.

Gouramma had often tried to discourage him from such activities but Girish would shrug off her lecture with a laugh. 'Amma, I don't agree with you. What Appa says is right. As a human being it is our duty to help everyone.'

Gouramma then usually directed her anger at her husband. 'Bad enough that you are impractical, you have now spoilt him and given him wrong ideas. How will he ever be a successful man with this sort of approach to life and society?'

Shamanna would pacify her. 'Leave him alone. Chandru will be the successful man you want your sons to be. This one will grow up to be like me, and if god is kind, he will get a good wife, like you are. Who, otherwise, will take care of him, us, and the house?'

Gouramma would shake her head but her anger would dissolve into the firmament.

Once news of Chandru's posting to the US was out, marriage proposals began to flood in. However, neither Chandru nor his mother was in favour of marriage at this stage. Their plan was that he should first go to America, settle down, work hard, and send money to add an upper storey to the modest one-storey house, then finance Surabhi's marriage.

It would make things much easier for the family since Shamanna was due to retire within a year. After all, they could not expect much from Girish, with his clerical job and modest income, so Gouramma had set her sights entirely on Chandru's earning potential. He was, in a way, the captain of the ship.

D-day came, and Chandru was about to leave for Florida on a one-year deputation. Surabhi had already given him a list of cosmetics, perfumes and chiffon saris that she wanted. Gouramma, on her part, had only said, 'Try to stay there as long as possible. If you stay long enough, I would like to join you.' Then, after a pause, had added, 'It seems you get nice cardamom and Spanish saffron.'

Girish and Shamanna made no demands whatsoever.

The dream, held dear for so long, had finally come true. Chandru arrived in the land of opportunities and amazing wealth.

Chandru was an intelligent, thinking man. He tended to compare the two countries, India and America. There were some things about the US that really appealed to him. America was rich, healthy and vibrant like a spirited youth, bursting with life. It was a nation forever on its toes. There were no words like powercuts or water shortages. Housing was easily available. He could find his way around anywhere with the help of a map—there was no need to thrust questions at strangers on the road. He could easily afford to buy a car and a house. The government was efficient and effective. All in all, this country was more than capable of fulfilling the basic needs of all its citizens and that is why it was the richest nation on earth and the most powerful.

By contrast, in India everything was a hassle. It was, no doubt, a five-thousand-year-old civilization where great kings like Ashoka and Harshavardana had ruled. The land that had been praised by poets and writers in the days of yore had now become home to scarcity and superstition. It was a body weakened by prolonged and painful disease, with its vital organs decayed, its essences sapped. It was not fair to compare the two countries. If one was the sky, the other was the earth. One was dark, the other incandescent light.

Chandru became enamoured of the comforts and charms of the American way of life very soon. How wonderful this country is! he would tell himself a thousand times. How happy the people living here are . . .

৵

Even his work was very satisfying, unlike the field visits he had had to make on the dusty roads of Dharwad. In order to improve his prospects, Chandru enrolled for computer classes in the evenings. His company agreed to pay for them. Chandru lived frugally and saved as much as he could. Because of the exchange rate even a hundred dollars meant at least four and a half thousand rupees. So, the hard working, ambitious, capable Chandru rapidly climbed the ladder of success. It filled him with ebullience, gave him a new zest for life.

But he did miss his family, especially when he returned home in the evenings. He would call his mother every weekend and describe his new American life, particularly how he went grocery shopping. He would describe the variety of juices packed in different kinds of bottles and cartons, the huge range of ice creams in all sorts of flavours and containers available in the stores, all the fruits and vegetables neatly packed and ready to eat . . . Often he would talk about garbage trucks, K-mart sales and money changing machines.

At first, when he did not have the heart to throw away empty bottles of juice or cans of milk, he would tell his mother, 'Amma, if you were here, you would have filled all these lovely bottles with varieties of pickles.'

Sometimes he would talk on different issues. 'Food is so cheap in America and people are so trustworthy and honest. They pick up newspapers from unmanned roadside stalls and diligently leave the money. There is no need for bus conductors on the buses. Each one pays the fare without being asked or told. No cheating.'

Then he would talk to Girish about the Dollar.

'The Dollar is the most powerful financial instrument of modern times. It is magic money. One dollar is equal to forty-two Indian rupees. If you have Dollars in your pocket, you can travel to any corner of the world without worry. It is universally acceptable currency.'

After a phone call from Chandru, Gouramma found it difficult to concentrate on the cooking. Often, the rice would be overcooked, the vegetables half-done, the dal would have too much salt and the coffee too much sugar. Gouramma was in India only in body at such times; her spirit would be flying across the length and breadth of America. She would dream about the Dollar, that magic green currency, which could change her house and fulfil her dreams. It was the Dollar, not Indian rupees, which could elevate her into the elite circle at social gatherings and marriage halls. The Dollar was like the Goddess Lakshmi, with a magic wand.

Before they knew it, Chandru had spent a year and a half in America. It was time for him to return home. The thought distressed him. His thoughts began to wander in a whole new direction. He had noticed that some of his senior colleagues had 'skipped', that is, taken employment in an American company without informing their original employers. The new employer assured them they would get an extension on the existing H1 visa or a green card, depending on the situation. These 'skippers' had signed bonds in India before leaving for America, promising to return and work for a minimum of three years in the parent organization.

Non-fulfilment of the bond invited penalties. But those who 'skipped' had scant regard for such 'petty' matters. The general attitude was, 'Let them trace us first and then penalize us. At that time we will see what is to be done.' Chandru had heard such stories ever since he had landed in America. It seemed to have become a fairly common trick. His colleagues Rajiv and Shrikant had signed bonds in India and had then gone underground in America. They were living in Colorado. The senior officers of Chandru's company had asked Chandru for their addresses. But though Chandru knew where Rajiv and Shrikant were, he remained silent.

Once they acquired the proper visa or green card, the holed-up 'skippers' boldly came out of their concealment, went home to India to marry pretty girls from rich, respectable families and returned in great style, to lead a happy and settled life. They became citizens of Dollar Country and their wives graduated and became 'Dollar Bahus'.

Chandru found himself thinking along these lines more often now. The more he thought, the more convinced he was that 'skipping' was the best thing to do. With the additional software skills that he had acquired, getting another job would not be difficult either. Of course, he could go back to India and take up a good software job there, but he wasn't ready to depart from this wondrous land of money and opportunities.

It did not take him long to make up his mind. He called his mother and explained that only with cooperation from his family members, by keeping things confidential, would he be successful in his plan, and that he would come to India only after he got a green card.

'Of course, we will keep it under wraps! Don't you worry about such things, just go ahead with your plans.

Thanks to the dollars that you have been sending, we are living much better. I do not want to face the same old difficulties again,' his mother told him quite frankly. More than helping her son in his plan, she was delighted that she could soon tell everyone that her elder son was an NRI.

Chandru began to scour the employment announcements. Soon, he saw an advertisement for a job with a company based in Nashville, Tennessee, near the East Coast. It was a state with a low density of population and beautiful cattle-grazing pastures. But Nashville was not a place many people wanted to go to. Winter temperatures were bone chilling at 53 °F and hence, despite the fat salaries, hardly anyone applied for jobs there. The new company promised to help Chandru acquire a green card. It was thus the right job at the right place for his period of hiding!

Without a word to anybody, Chandru sold his car, packed his bags and, leaving the lights on in the house allotted to him by his former employers, simply 'disappeared'. When his Florida boss made enquiries a week later, he discovered that Chandru had vanished.

Whenthe bus to Jayanagar arrived, overflowing with passengers, Vinuta became frantic. If she missed this bus, then she would be almost an hour late for her job at the school, and that was as good as half a day's leave. Her job was temporary and she could not afford leave without pay. With great pushing and shoving, Vinuta managed to get into the bus. Actually, she disliked doing this, but in a place like Bangalore, she had no choice.

She leaned on the metal pole flushed with the pride of a victor. The bus conductor asked her where she wanted to go. 'Jayanagar,' she said as she fumbled in her purse for change. But all she found was the hundred-rupee note that she had received from the private tuition she was giving. She held out the note. The conductor was most irritated. 'I don't have change even for five rupees, where will I get it for a hundred? Anyway tell your husband to buy the ticket.' The old conductor had got her married in a fraction of a second, without spending a single rupee! Vinuta turned around and saw a tall young man just behind her, smiling and handing over the change to the conductor, saying, 'Jayanagar, two please.'

The conductor laughed knowingly. 'Your husband has the change and you wanted to get change from me?'

'What husband?' Vinuta shot out, but her question was lost in the swirl of packed humanity. She spoke sternly to the tall man. 'Listen, sir, I will pay you my fare the minute we disembark.'

'Quite all right,' the young man said. 'No problem.'

'For you it's not a problem. But I cannot accept a free ticket from anybody,' she said firmly. Vinuta got off at the bus stop to walk to the school where she worked. This had been her routine now for the past several months, commuting every day from her aunt's house in Rajajinagar to the school in Jayanagar.

The beautiful Dharwad days had come to an unexpected, abrupt end. Uncle Bheemanna had died suddenly of a heart attack. The family had dispersed, leaving only Seetakka, the grandmother, and Vinuta in Dharwad. Later, even Seetakka went away to stay with her other children but no one was prepared to take the responsibility of supporting Vinuta. She was of marriageable age, with no money of her own and no place to go to. Fortunately, her aunt, Indu, and her husband, Rama Rao, generously offered their support. Indu had said, 'Bangalore is a big city. You will soon get a job. Once you have a job, it will be easy to get you married. When the marriage is fixed, you can sell the Dharwad house and cover the marriage expenses. For the time being, you can rent it out and keep your things in the upper-storey room.'

Vinuta felt miserable. She implored, 'Please let us not sell the house. That is the last remembrance of my parents. I love that garden. My life is in that . . .'

'Vinuta, be practical, child. You cannot afford to be sentimental at this time,' consoled Indu. 'Of course, if you find a prince charming who will agree to marry you without any money, then you won't need to give up the house.'

Vinuta was distraught. Every tree, every corner, every fragrance, even in the deep dark night, held so many memories, so much happiness. But Indu was right. Vinuta caressed all the plants of her garden and tearfully bid them goodbye. With a heavy heart, she reached Bangalore.

Though she had a BEd degree she knew she would not get a job right away. So she started giving music lessons at home until she got a temporary job in a school in Jayanagar . . .

She had walked a few steps when Vinuta realized she had to pay the man for her ticket. She turned round and saw him right behind her.

'My name is Girish. I work in the Jayanagar branch of Canara Bank,' he said and smiled.

'Just give me two minutes. I will get change,' she told him.

Where would she get the change, since none of the shops were open, he thought to himself. But he said nothing. He wanted to see what this self-willed girl would do.

Vinuta returned after a while, crestfallen. 'You said you work for a bank. Please, take this hundred-rupee note and get change for me. I will come and collect it later.'

Girish was taken aback. 'But . . . but . . . what is your name?' he asked.

'Vinuta Desai. I am a teacher in that school.' She pointed towards the school nearby. 'I must go now. I am getting late.' She gave him the note and with a polite smile, walked away.

Girish stared after her, wondering at her behaviour, as she walked out of sight.

Only after she reached the school did Vinuta realize what she had done. How could she have trusted an unknown man with a hundred rupees, for which she had worked hard all month, merely on the basis of him saying he worked in a bank? Why had she assumed he was speaking the truth? How could she have been so impulsive?

At the end of the day, she walked to the bank with her fingers crossed. She could not even remember whether his name was Girish or Ramesh.

Sudha Murty

Girish was waiting for her outside the bank. 'If you hadn't come, I would have come to your school and returned the money,' he said politely.

Vinuta was greatly relieved. 'Do you know someone in that school?'

'I know Shamanna Master very well. I would have sent the money through him if you hadn't come today. Here is your money.'

'Thank you,' she said, with a smile, noticing that he had put it in an envelope.

In the bus, she opened the envelope and saw it contained change for a full hundred rupees. Girish had not deducted the bus fare!

✍

About a week later, while Vinuta was helping her aunt in the kitchen, her aunt said, 'Vinu, this Sunday, take a holiday from your music class.'

'Why?'

'Some people are coming to see you. A marriage proposal. They are not rich people. From Bangalore only. The boy is a clerk in a bank. He has an elder brother in America who will come to India only after two years. That is why they are planning the second son's marriage. They also have a daughter, yet to be married off. Are you particular that you only want an engineer or a class I officer or something?'

'No. I don't have any such demands. Nor am I bothered about his family's riches. If necessary, I will continue to work. All I ask for is to be contented.' That was what Vinuta really felt and what she honestly believed.

After seeing Vinuta in the bus and later discovering that she worked in the same school as his father, Girish had become quite interested in her. Though Gouramma had no plans of getting Girish married before Chandru, her elder son had clearly told her that he couldn't say when he would get his green card, so they should not delay Girish's marriage for his sake.

That was when Gouramma had started inviting proposals from parents of marriageable girls.

One evening, Girish casually asked his father, 'How is that teacher Vinuta Desai, who works in your school?'

'She is a very nice girl. And she has an excellent voice. She is from Dharwad, but of our own community. Why? How do you know her?'

Girish told him about the incident on the bus.

When Girish had gone out, Shamanna said to his wife, 'Gouri, I think Girish is interested in that girl. It will be a good match. Should we make some enquiries?'

'No, certainly not. We are the boy's side, let her elders approach us,' said the arrogant mother of an eligible boy.

However, Shamanna had other ideas. And his secret plans worked.

He and his family went to see the girl.

Girish did not know who the girl was, and had gone along quite reluctantly.

On their way, Surabhi teased him, 'Girish, Appa says it is very hard to say no to this girl. All these days you had only one teacher. If you marry her, you will have two teachers at home.'

'Who told you all this?' Girish was impatient.

'Appa. He said Vinuta Desai is working in the school where he is . . .'

Girish's face brightened noticeably. In fact, it was hard to hide his joy.

Both Gouramma and Surabhi liked Vinuta in their very first meeting. She looked very pleasant, and the kind who would be willing to adjust. Shamanna had been in favour of this alliance right from the start and Girish was more than happy.

Vinuta too felt she was fortunate and was willing to agree instantly.

Before Shamanna and his family left, Rama Rao explained Vinuta's financial constraints. 'If you let me know your decision as soon as possible, it will help us. We will have enough time to make arrangements to sell the house.'

At those words, Vinuta's face fell, and Girish was sensitive enough to notice it at once.

Chandru took up the job in Nashville and settled down there quickly. His company sponsored him for a green card, but his lawyer told him that it was difficult to say exactly how long it would take—anything from a month to several years.

Chandru's life went on, each day bringing renewed hope of the much-awaited green card. Almost two years and a half had gone by and there was as yet no sign of the green card. Chandru missed India and his family. Some people he knew had managed to get their green cards. Immediately they had returned to India with the sole intent of getting married. They would see thirty potential brides in twenty days and then at the end of the whirlwind campaign get married in the matter of a week, with neither of the spouses knowing anything about the other. Some of the young men would take the pains to look at several proposals, shortlist them, meet a few and then decide. Many had even decided on a particular bride purely on the basis of a photo or video.

Lately, Chandru's fascination for the American lifestyle had waned. He had begun to take for granted the comforts and facilities that had earlier filled him with such awe. He had become increasingly lonely and wanted to get married as soon as possible. Besides, his ambition, the obsession to work in America, earn in dollars, attain a good standard of living and then get a green card, was almost achieved. His mind, so far filled only with that one thought, was free to consider other alternatives. Matrimony was an attractive, rather pleasant option.

The thought of marriage reminded him of Vinuta. For some time, he had completely forgotten about her. He had really liked her, but marriage had been far from his mind then. Now that he wanted to get married, she occupied his thoughts once more. But he did not know whether his feelings were reciprocated. Besides, she may even have got married by this time!

One night, he seriously considered expressing his feelings for her through a letter. He worried about what her response would be, but then, impulse won over caution and he wrote:

Dear Vinuta,

You will be surprised to receive this letter. Please do not misread my intentions. I have been in America for the last few years. I have always appreciated your good qualities. If you have similar feelings about me, kindly let me know. I can't come back to India without a green card. If you are sure and can wait for me, I will talk to your uncle and to my parents. You will find my address on the cover.

If you do not have any such feelings, then just destroy this letter and the chapter will be closed.

With regards,
Chandru

Several days passed, and he heard nothing from Vinuta. His imagination started going haywire. Someone else may have opened the letter and the whole of Dharwad had heard about it, or she might be married and her husband may have opened the letter . . . He broke out in a sweat, feeling that he had probably put her in a difficult situation and cursed himself for his foolishness.

Finally, a month and a half later, he got a response: His letter had come back stamped 'Addressee not found'. Chandru just tore up the letter and killed the dream in his heart.

Gouramma started the pre-marriage talks. 'After all, this is the first wedding in our family and we have to invite all our relatives and friends . . . We do not want any dowry, but everybody will be keen to know what saris and jewellery Vinuta will wear . . . Our elder son is in America and we have to maintain our status, isn't it? If the wedding is simple, like that of ten other people, we will be ridiculed . . . The wedding should be grand . . . If the house were in Bangalore, it would have been a different thing. What will we do with a house in Dharwad? It is better that she sells the house . . .'

At this point, Shamanna had enough. He could no longer hold back his displeasure at his wife's words. 'Gouri, we should not interfere in this. Leave it to Girish and Vinuta. Selling a house just for the sake of a show-off wedding is foolish. You know as well as I do what a struggle it is to build a house. We have been able to build the first floor only because Chandru is in America and is sending us money in dollars. Till then we had been living in a small house.'

Gouramma's face reflected the anger she felt at her husband's remarks. To prevent further argument, Girish intervened. 'I will talk to Vinuta and we will decide. Leave it to us.'

Girish and Vinuta met at a restaurant close to her house. Though Girish was normally outgoing and talkative, that evening he was tongue-tied, hunting for words to start a conversation. Vinuta, naturally shy, waited eagerly for him to speak.

Sudha Murty

'How is your house in Dharwad? Is it big?' Girish asked abruptly.

'Oh! It is not just a house, my whole life, my heart is in it.' Vinuta's eyes sparkled. 'I love it so much that at times I feel I cannot give it up. But I don't have the money to arrange a grand marriage . . .' Her eyes filled with tears.

Girish smiled and affectionately took hold of her hands. 'If it is so painful for you, we will not sell the house. Let's have a simple wedding. Amma may get upset for some time and she might scold you or taunt us, but we will put up with it. We should not start our new life with tears. My mother is actually a very nice person, good at heart but sometimes she can act rather tough. She softens up later.'

Vinuta was deeply touched by Girish's words. She could not speak, but tears of gratitude flowed down her cheeks.

A few days later Gouramma called Chandru and gave him the news.

'Girish is engaged to be married. The girl is a teacher in Appa's school. I really wish you could come for the wedding. We will postpone the date until you can come. Ideally, you should have got married before Girish. But since you told us about your green card problem, we have decided to go ahead with Girish's wedding . . . Chandru, the first floor of the house is finally completed. We all are so grateful to you. Without your help, we would have never seen any of these comforts . . .'

Chandru did not bother to ask for the details of his brother's bride. He was almost certain that the girl had been chosen by his father. Though he liked his brother Girish and was happy that he was getting married, he felt it was not practical to fly down to India just to be present for the ceremony. He chose instead to send them a gift of five hundred dollars. Knowing his mother, he was quite sure that the money would matter more than his presence.

Chandru was now more conversant with the language of the Dollar. He wrote out a cheque. This was the first rung of success. Chandru was mighty satisfied and contented that he had climbed that rung of American life. The thought of returning to India had receded to the back of his mind. Somehow, living in the same small house, sharing the toilet and bathroom with others, having to breathe polluted air, and finding dirt and dust all around seemed most disagreeable to him.

Vinuta was very happy in her new house. Shamanna reminded her of her uncle Bheemanna, only a better-educated version.

Girish lavished love on her. She realized her mother-in-law was a domineering person and Surabhi a carefree, easy-going, rather self-centred person. All these years, she had been the only girl in the family but now with the arrival of Vinuta, Surabhi looked upon her as a rival, a competitor, for the family's affections.

Unlike Vinuta, Surabhi was quite immature and looked upon life as a series of shopping expeditions for jewels and clothes, and outings for movies with friends. These represented to her the essence of a good life. She was not interested in studying for a postgraduate degree, nor was she concerned about staying at home all day without taking responsibility for any housework. If she chose to stay at home, her time was spent gossiping with her mother and watching TV serials in the afternoons.

Gouramma indulged her fully, treating her like a princess. 'Leave the poor girl alone. After all, she will marry one of these days and the responsibilities will begin. At least until then let her enjoy life,' she would say if Shamanna or Girish asked Surabhi to do something.

Vinuta, however, took on many of the household chores soon after she joined the family. She would wake up early and help her mother-in-law in the morning before going to school. She now had a permanent job in the same government school. Sometimes, she felt a little sad that Girish did not have an ear for music, like Shamanna did. But he certainly did not object to her singing.

Shamanna would often say, 'Vinu, you have a good voice. You should pursue music as an alternative career.'

Shashikala was one of the temporary teachers in Vinuta's school. Over the months she and Vinuta had become really close friends. One day, Shashi came to school, beaming. 'Vinuta,' she said in a low voice, 'I have some news to give you. Let us go out for lunch.'

During the lunch break she said with a blush, 'My marriage has been fixed. With Shankar. His father and mine are great friends.'

'Oh, that's very good news! Congratulations! So, what does he do? Where is he from?'

'Shankar is an MA in English and works as a part-time lecturer in a college in Mysore. He is also doing his PhD. After marriage, we plan to open tutorials. We will surely get on very well because we have known each other since childhood.'

'Oh, that is good. When are you resigning?'

'I am giving my letter next week because I have to give two months' notice to the school. Shankar's family do not have the custom of engagement in their family. So it will be the wedding, direct, in three months. It's going to be in Mysore.'

'Wish you all the best,' Vinuta said again as she shook Shashi's hands warmly.

Vinuta missed Shashikala a great deal when she left the school, but involved herself totally in her work; it made her less lonely. Vinuta was really looking forward to Shashikala's wedding. Since she and Girish had started life together, the two of them had never gone out anywhere except to a temple or the vegetable market. Now for the first time she would be going out of town with her husband.

One day, out of the blue, the headmistress, Sushila Rao, called Vinuta to her office. 'It seems Shashi's marriage has been cancelled. Do you have any idea why? You ought to know because you two are great friends.'

Vinuta was shocked. 'I didn't know this,' she replied. Sushila continued to talk about Shashi, but Vinuta did not hear anything. Her mind was in a tortured spin. What could have happened? Had there been an accident? This was a marriage fixed with the approval of both sets of parents, so what could possibly have gone wrong?

Somehow Vinuta managed to finish her work for the day and hurried to Shashi's house. Shashi opened the door. When she saw Vinuta, she simply broke down.

Vinuta looked around and noticed that the marriage preparations, which had been going on in full swing, had been stopped midway.

Shashi's mother came into the room. 'Vinuta,' she said, 'you are Shashi's friend, tell her not to act like this. She hasn't eaten for two days. It's destiny. She was not meant to marry Shankar. What to do!'

Shashi took Vinuta's hand and walked up to the terrace. It was pleasantly cool, all the lights in the city were gradually coming on. Vinuta marvelled at the beautiful sight, but to Shashi, nothing mattered. Vinuta put her arm around Shashi's shoulders and gently asked, 'What happened? Is Shankar all right? Has he met with an accident or something?'

In an instant, grief vanished from Shashi's face. A seething fury replaced it.

'What can possibly happen to him? That devil is rock solid. He has humiliated all of us. I am just sick of life. I gave my heart to an unworthy man.'

'Don't talk in riddles. Tell me straight, what happened?'

'He sold himself,' Shashi said savagely. 'One Indian family settled in the US came to India in search of a groom for their daughter. They put an ad in the papers saying that the girl had a green card and wanted a groom with certain qualifications.'

'And Shankar fell for the proposal?' Vinuta asked in disbelief.

'He was not alone. Many others, doctors, CAs and other professionals, also applied, and went, just as if for a job interview. But Shankar was selected because the girl was also an MA in Literature. They offered him a green card through marriage and to support his PhD studies at any university in the US.'

'But what about you?'

'Who cares for me? His parents feel it is a great opportunity for him. He now feels that there is no future in tutorials. He has two sisters to be married off and his father is a retired man. If he had stayed back in India and married me, we would both have had to slog all our lives to repay the loans.' After a pause, Shashi added, 'Shankar told me that he would cover half my marriage expenses once he went to America. How generous of him, don't you think?'

'But Shashi, you have resigned your job and everyone knows about your marriage. Is nobody worried about that?'

'What's a teacher's job, a simple girl's life, in front of the Dollar?'

Vinuta was speechless.

Chandru's dream had come true. He had finally got the magic ticket to the gates of heaven, the glorious green card. He was settled for life now. The son of an ordinary schoolmaster, who had never dreamed of riches, had not just become rich, he was now also an official resident of America.

He was on top of the world.

When he came home that evening he found a letter from Bangalore. Normally, he talked to his parents over the phone and rarely exchanged letters, so he guessed it was a long list of Surabhi's demands or some such thing. He freshened up, brewed himself a cup of coffee and sat on the sofa to open the envelope.

It was a letter from Girish with a few pictures enclosed.

Dear Chandru,

It would have been great if you could have attended our simple wedding. Anyway, I have sent some photos. Vinu says she knows you and has conveyed her regards to you.

With affection,
Girish

Chandru looked at the photos. HIS Vinu, the same girl with the golden voice, had become his brother's wife!

Something that he had never imagined was now a harsh reality. The spring goddess of Dharwad, the girl who had stolen his heart, the Jayanagar schoolteacher were all the same girl. What a coincidence! What irony!

The joy and excitement of that evening evaporated. For a minute, he was upset with himself: if he had not waited for the green card and had returned to India earlier, he could have married Vinuta. Then, he was jealous. Girish was neither handsome nor as well placed as he was, but had won a wife who was far superior to him in everything.

He looked at the photos once again. Vinuta looked radiant.

It took a few days for Chandru to accept what had happened and digest the reality of life.

The house was bustling with activity and anticipation. Chandru was due to come home after almost six years. Vinuta too shared the excitement. When she had set foot in Girish's house after the wedding, she had learnt that Girish's brother, who lived in the US, had been their tenant in Dharwad. That was when she had seen Chandru's photos in her new home and recognized him. She then remembered his love for music and his diffidence in praising her openly. Providence had made him her brother-in-law, who deserved her respect and regard.

Now, as she decorated the house for his welcome, she wondered, would Chandru remember her as the girl from Dharwad, whose singing he had praised? Would he ask her to sing again? Gouramma, Girish and Surabhi got ready to go to the airport to receive Chandru. Shamanna was happy that his son was coming home after so long, but was not very keen on going to the airport. 'Let me stay home and prepare to welcome him. Anyway, there will be no space for me on the way back. His luggage will need all the space,' he joked.

Vinuta had told her mother-in-law earlier, 'Amma, you go to the airport. Tell me what Chandru likes and I will get everything ready.' Gouramma really liked Vinuta's attitude: totally unselfish and willing to adjust to any situation. She went to the airport confident that Vinuta would take care of everything at home to welcome Chandru.

Gouramma's eyes filled with tears, at the first sight of her son after six long years. Her heart swelled with pride, to see him healthier and altogether more handsome. Chandru walked up to his mother, dragging two huge suitcases, and bent down to touch her feet. It was a touching moment.

When they reached home, Chandru went straight to his father and bowed down to touch his father's feet. He then saw Vinuta standing near the door.

'How are you? Do you remember me?' His voice had mellowed.

'I am fine. How was your journey?' Vinuta smiled amiably.

He saw that the teenage Vinu of Dharwad had now matured into a young woman. Her face glowed with the happiness and contentment in her soul. She probably got everything here that she had missed in Dharwad.

Even before he had a wash and could sit down, he saw his mother and sister struggling to open his suitcases. With a sigh, he opened it for them and unpacked everything: the digital camera and video, cosmetics, perfumes, walnuts, saffron, chocolates, handbags, chiffon saris . . . the whole lot of goodies that they had been hankering for.

Surabhi was engrossed in checking out her list. Handing over a bunch of hundred-dollar notes to Gouramma, Chandru said, 'Amma, I could not do much shopping for everyone. Please buy whatever you feel is right.' Gouramma took the money, speechless.

'I have already eaten on the plane. I just want to rest for a while. Didn't sleep at all on the flight,' Chandru said, moving towards the stairs to the first floor.

Gouramma was in seventh heaven. A woman who had never been able to indulge herself and had struggled all her life to make ends meet, was now swimming in a sea of opulence. A thousand dollars, when converted into rupees, was a lot of money. But sharing had never been part of her nature. She was mentally listing all the things that she could buy . . .

After Chandru's arrival, Gouramma seemed to forget the kitchen. She wanted to spend every possible minute with her son. Vinuta cheerfully took over all the responsibilities. She understood the feelings of a mother who was meeting her son after such a long time. She also made sure she served snacks and coffee to the numerous guests who dropped in to meet Chandru. She had, in fact, taken leave from her work for that period. Surabhi, on the other hand, when she was at home, was completely preoccupied with the mirror, trying on all the new American cosmetics, or she accompanied Chandru almost everywhere he went.

Chandru had come home for just three weeks. He wanted to meet his old friends and colleagues. He would have liked to meet his former employer, but he was too embarrassed. His conscience still pricked him for 'skipping'. He had cheated on a company that had financed his trip and paid for his computer training. But he quickly scotched his inner voice. He rationalized that he was not the only one: several brilliant young men from his poor country had done the same thing to settle in the land of opportunity.

As soon as word got round that Shamanna's son was in India, marriage proposals began to pour in. He was a prize catch. Gouramma had shortlisted four girls for Chandru to choose from. One shrewd father, Krishnappa, was a property developer. He had a daughter and a son. He owned a palatial house and three cars. His eye fell on Chandru. When he came to visit Gouramma, he quickly gauged the situation. If the greedy Gouramma was lured, then there would be no problem in finalizing the match. He invited them to his farmhouse.

Gouramma was thrilled. She went eagerly to see them. Krishnappa and his wife Parvati flaunted their silverware and gold and diamond jewellery, calculated to impress. Their daughter, Jamuna, was an ordinary graduate and spent her time going for painting, ikebana or batik classes. Had it not been for her dusky complexion she would have got even more eligible, good-looking and well-settled grooms. Her visits to beauty clinics had been fruitless. But in an expensive sari, bedecked with jewels, she looked very appealing to Gouramma that day.

Jamuna was effusively friendly with Surabhi and that made Gouramma very comfortable. When they were leaving, Parvati handed over baskets of vegetables and fruits, saying, 'The match is not in our hands. But let us at least continue with the cordial relationship.' Gouramma left with tears in her eyes.

On the way home, Gouramma silently prayed that her son would choose Jamuna as his bride, and began enumerating her virtues. In the end Shamanna was forced to say, 'Let Chandru decide.'

In his heart, Shamanna felt that a bride coming from such a family, used to a wealthy lifestyle, would normally have a large ego. He doubted if she would fit into his middle-class family.

A few days later, Krishnappa sent his car to pick up Chandru. Chandru went alone. In the light of the chandelier, Jamuna's diamond studs sparkled. After some initial small talk, Chandru came to the point. 'I want to be clear about some things. We are from a middle-class family, and as the eldest of the family, I have responsibilities.'

Jamuna was equally forthright. Bluntly she asked him, 'Do you plan to settle down in America or do you mean to return sometime?'

'Well, I plan to settle there. But one should be aware that life in America is lonely, as against life in India.'

'One can always make friends.'

'You are the only daughter. If you want to come to visit your parents, it may be very expensive.'

'Oh, that should not be a problem. If I can't come, they will visit us.'

Chandru had seen some of his friends' wives going into depression due to loneliness, particularly in the smaller towns in the US. He wanted a bold girl who could face life and enjoy it there. He was not particularly keen on marrying a working girl, although it would be the girl's decision whether to work there or not. He was aware that he had no family support there, as he had in India. So he wanted to be absolutely sure and he wanted the girl he married to know exactly what the situation was.

As far as Jamuna was concerned, his mother had done the preliminary enquiries. She looked satisfactory and was quite clear-headed and outgoing. Chandru gave the green signal after some thought.

જ

It had been almost ten days since Chandru's return to India. The long stay away from India made him feel quite disoriented. The country had changed so much, he thought. Swelling crowds, dustier, dirtier streets, hectic construction activity all round, there was hardly a vacant site in the neighbourhood. Pollution in the air, in the water, in the food was taking its toll on him. As a result, he suffered from an upset stomach and constant pain. A college friend, Ravichandra, had become a doctor and had a clinic near his house. Chandru went to consult him. Ravi was very happy to see him. While examining Chandru he casually asked him what he was doing.

'Chandru, your stomach has become very sensitive. You must have eaten enough home food to make up the deficit of all these years in just one visit. Your stomach cannot handle all that spicy and rich stuff your mother is serving you.'

Ravi wrote out a prescription and jokingly said, 'Chandru, a software engineer's life is any day better than a doctor's. To finally become specialists we spend ten years or more after pre-university. Whereas software engineers spend four years studying and earn more than a doctor earns. And that is particularly true since you are in America. Your dollar salary, when multiplied forty-three times in India, is a huge amount of money.'

'I agree. The market is like that. But it is not easy in America either. Anyway, what is your fee?' Chandru cut short the conversation.

'How can I take money from you? You are a friend.'

But Chandru insisted, and reluctantly Ravi said, 'Three hundred rupees.'

Chandru paid it and came home. The next day, when asking Girish to encash some traveller's cheques, Chandru casually said, 'It seems India has become very expensive. I didn't know doctors charge so much these days. I feel like Rip Van Winkle.'

Girish was surprised. 'Why, what happened?'

'Ravi took three hundred rupees from me as consultation fees.'

'What! Ravi normally charges hundred and fifty rupees. Two days ago I had taken a colleague of mine to him.'

Without waiting for Chandru's reaction, Girish rushed off to his bank.

It was Chandru's first taste of the double-fare formula.

Chandru's wedding with Jamuna was set for the following week. The house was bursting with a new energy. Chandru hired a taxi for easy mobility in the days leading up to the wedding.

He gave his mother four thousand dollars for wedding expenses. Gouramma had never seen that kind of money in all her life. She was effervescent with joy. She explained her plans to Chandru. 'Jamuna is from a rich family. We should give her nice saris and jewels for the wedding. Otherwise they will look down upon us.'

'Amma, don't buy too many saris for Jamuna. In America, she will rarely get a chance to wear them. I would suggest that the three of you buy yourselves expensive saris that will be done due justice during festivals and functions.'

Gouramma, Surabhi and Chandru went sari shopping. As usual, Vinuta was left to take care of the preparations at home. In the sari shop, Surabhi was enjoying herself, asking the salesman to pull out saris of unusual combinations and varieties. Greedy Gouramma was at another counter making her choices. Chandru quietly asked the salesman to show him an aquamarine sari with a pink border.

When he saw the sari, he told his mother to buy it for Girish's wife and not for Jamuna. Gouramma took a look at the price tag: it was seven thousand rupees.

'Chandru, she doesn't wear such expensive saris. It would be wiser to buy two printed silk saris for the same amount.'

But Chandru insisted on the sari he had selected, and Gouramma backed down. He was paying the bill after all.

Chandru reasoned that when Vinuta had taken such good care of him when he was not so well off, social restrictions had held him back from gifting her a sari of her choice. But now, when an appropriate occasion was coming up, he could repay what he felt was a long-held personal debt.

Vinuta took one look at the sari and her face lit up like a flower in full bloom. She murmured, 'Oh! I love this colour. I have been planning to buy one for a long time. Thank you very much, Chandru.'

Gouramma felt she had to give Jamuna something from the family. Shamanna was not a wealthy man. So Gouramma took two of her own bangles to a jeweller and got them redesigned into new ones. Vinuta's sharp eyes noticed this.

As the wedding date drew near, a whole lot of relatives and friends started visiting their house. Gouramma enjoyed herself, boosting her own self-esteem, showing off Jamuna's jewels and saris, humiliating them, destroying their peace of mind, paying them back for every insult she believed she had suffered for so many years. Her son lived in America and her future daughter-in-law was the only daughter of a rich man. Such charming scenarios, mere dreams for so long, were gloriously coming true. In her mind she thanked the blessed power of the Dollar.

Krishnappa was a wealthy man. He wanted to use the wedding ceremony to display his wealth and exploit this occasion as a business party. So, the most expensive hall was selected as the venue for three days of grand celebrations. The hall was decorated with the choicest flowers, live music was played throughout the ceremony and the affluent guests, especially the ladies, flaunted their silks and jewels. Of course, the wide spread of rich food was the gravitation point for all appetites.

From behind the scenes, Girish and Vinuta ensured that everything went off without a hitch. But it was Gouramma who handled all money-related matters.

After the wedding, Jamuna's mother made a dramatic appeal to Gouramma. 'Please consider Jamuna as your daughter. She has been brought up in luxury. If she makes any mistake, kindly forgive her. If there has been any lapse in the marriage arrangements from our side, please pardon us.' With that, she handed over an expensive gift to Gouramma. Gouramma was overcome with emotion and hugged Jamuna's mother fondly.

Chandru and Jamuna went off for their honeymoon and returned just one day before Chandru's departure for the US. That evening, Chandru said to his mother, 'Amma, Jamuna will stay with you until she gets her visa, and I shall only be back here for Surabhi's wedding. Till then, take care.'

'Jamuna is my eldest daughter-in-law. It is, after all, her own house now. Let her get used to us. You needn't worry about her,' Gouramma reassured Chandru.

The day Chandru left, Jamuna politely told her mother-in-law, 'My cousins are all at my parents' place. I want to spend some time with them before flying off. I will be back next week.' From the airport Jamuna went straight to her father's house.

Gouramma realized that she could not boss over Jamuna the way she did over Vinuta. She told herself it was all right. Her rich relatives had come from all over and there was nothing wrong in Jamuna's decision to go to her parents' home.

'Come back any time. This is your home too after all,' she said cordially.

But Jamuna simply vanished from their lives for a long time.

When she eventually did show up it was to tell the family, 'I am leaving for America tomorrow. I really feel very sorry that I could not spend time with you and Surabhi. I knew that the visa would take a long time, and so I went to meet all my uncles and aunts in Chennai, Delhi and Ahmedabad. The next time I come, I shall stay for a good three months with you.'

Shamanna had seen through Jamuna's pretence, but Gouramma, blinded by the dollars that her daughter-in-law now represented, reassured her. 'It is all right, my dear. I know that you are very fond of all of us. When Surabhi gets married, it will be your responsibility to see to everything. You are the "Mahalakshmi" of our house. You should not leave in sorrow. Go and join your husband in happiness. Our blessings shall be with you always.'

Jamuna did not even bother to talk to Vinuta. For that matter, nobody in the house seemed to even acknowledge her presence these days.

After Chandru's wedding, things took a different turn in the Shamanna household. Gouramma's conversations usually began with, 'Our Jamuna, in America . . .' Every day, she would repeat that they were very lucky to have such a daughter-in-law. Paeans of praise were constantly chanted for the unknown and absent Jamuna, and the two daughters-in-law were constantly compared.

Before Jamuna's advent into their lives Gouramma used to say, 'Now that Vinuta is here, I am totally relaxed, like a retired person. She takes care of everything.' But now, there was no such talk. The proverb, 'If you have money, like the sun you will shine; if you don't have money, like a dog you will whine', was quite apt in this case. Jamuna's sun shone brighter each day while Vinuta's life became more like that of a dog.

Whenever a guest or a relative came visiting, Jamuna was praised to the sky and the lavish wedding described in great detail. Photo albums and videos were forced upon the visitors. The entire list of presents given by Jamuna's family was recited. Her 'simplicity' and other assorted virtues were extolled. Gouramma even justified Jamuna having kept all the wedding gifts in her parents' house. 'Our house is so small. There is no space to keep all the gifts.'

Shamanna would walk away from such talk but where could poor Vinuta go?

Things became worse with the arrival of pictures from America sent by Jamuna. Jamuna's letters were a treatise on the American lifestyle, what she wore, where she went, the décor of the house, the car they drove and the places they visited. The day Jamuna called, Gouramma's mind sprouted wings. Surabhi was entranced. Vinuta however would get upset for she knew that the ill winds would blow harder.

⋘

It was a Saturday and all Vinuta's colleagues had decided to go for the noon show of *Veer Zara*. As Vinuta sat in the darkened cinema hall, a wave of nostalgia swept over her. She remembered the last time she had seen a movie at Dharwad's Regal theatre. Her entire college group had cut classes and gone for the morning show of *Mughal-e-Azam*. After the movie, Vinuta had practised singing the famous song 'Mohabbat ki jhoothi kahani pe roye' in the ladies' room. The next day, someone had written on the blackboard in their classroom, 'We do not want class today. We want to hear and see our own Madhubala singing "Mohabbat ki jhoothi kahani pe roye".'

Where were all those friends now and where had those magical times gone?

The bell rang signalling intermission, bringing Vinuta back to the present. She went out to buy popcorn for everybody. Suddenly her eyes caught sight of a pair of youngsters sipping a soft drink in a far corner of the balcony. Vinuta felt as if a hammer had hit her head. It was Surabhi and Gopinath.

Vinuta blinked to confirm that she was not dreaming.

Gopinath, a young, handsome neighbourhood boy was an old student of Shamanna's and now worked as a medical representative. His father was a postmaster and they lived in a small house nearby. Gopinath was an outgoing, friendly sort of person who was actively involved in all neighbourhood functions and festivities. So he had come to the house a few times with Girish. But Vinuta could not imagine that Surabhi and Gopinath were seeing each other.

She knew that Gouramma was looking for a suitable boy for Surabhi but she had too many conditions: He had to be handsome, rich, but should not be the only son, because then the in-laws would permanently live with their son. Neither should he have sisters because they would frequently visit their parents along with their families. It was better if he was one of two sons, preferably the younger. If there was no mother-in-law, it would be a bonus. They must own a car and a house. Preference would be given if the boy was living abroad.

But Surabhi was quite plain looking and not from a rich family. She was not a software engineer and hence many potential grooms who came from abroad rejected her.

Vinuta and Girish had even registered Surabhi's name with a marriage bureau and continuously scanned the matrimonial ads. Though Shamanna tried to tell his wife that one couldn't get a made-to-order husband, it was in vain.

Vinuta could not concentrate on the movie any more. What should she do? Tell the people at home or talk to Surabhi in private? But knowing Surabhi's and Gouramma's nature, she was scared.

She felt it was better to tell Shamanna, who was more mature in such matters. During the movie, she kept an eye on them and after that, she went straight home, but Surabhi had not yet reached.

She asked Shamanna, 'Where is Surabhi?'

'She has gone for ikebana class,' Shamanna answered in all innocence.

Gouramma was away at the temple and Girish was at work. Vinuta lowered her voice and said, 'I saw Surabhi with Gopinath at the cinema. I saw them with my own eyes and I felt they are more than friends. You should talk to Surabhi and find out. Anyway, we are looking for a boy for her, but if she is interested in this boy, then we should stop searching . . .'

Vinuta stopped abruptly when she saw Gouramma who had come in and had been quietly listening to her. Gouramma's face was pale.

Gouramma could not sleep that night. First, she was unhappy that her daughter had betrayed her and, second, that Vinuta had found out. She wanted Surabhi to settle down in the US and lead a life of luxury so that she could boast in front of everybody that two of her children were living abroad. Gopi was nowhere in her scheme of things.

Shamanna's views were different. Gopi was a well-behaved boy from a respectable middle-class family and it would be a good match. Surabhi would stay nearby.

Surabhi was unaware of all this. Gopi was her senior at college and she was attracted to his charming personality and easy manner. She knew that her mother would certainly object and so they would meet outside once in a while. But she had never thought of marrying him.

The following day Gouramma called her daughter and admonished her. 'Surabhi, you do not know how hard life is. Yesterday I came to know that you had gone for a movie with Gopi. What does he have? An ordinary job and a small house! If you marry him, your life will be like Vinuta's. You will have to count every penny and try to save all the time. Look at Jamuna! She has two cars; she can spend money in lakhs because she has money in dollars. The Dollar is all-powerful. You know it is the Dollar that has changed our lives! Have you not seen the photos of your brother's house? You can lead that kind of life if you marry someone who is in the US or someone very rich in India.'

Vinuta was in the kitchen. She heard this conversation and was utterly flabbergasted. Should a marriage be arranged on the basis of love and understanding or on the love for the Dollar, she wondered.

Alarmed by the Gopi incident, Gouramma expedited the search for a son-in-law. She would tell the matrimonial agent, 'We are ready to give a lavish wedding but we want a very good boy.' People would laugh behind her back and say, 'Gouramma is crazy. Five years ago she was nobody. Today she talks about a lavish wedding. She is searching for a groom only from the upper strata. As if people in America are the only possible match for her daughter!'

Vinuta noticed that after the incident Gouramma and Surabhi were very aloof and offhand with her.

One day Lakshman Rao, the matchmaker, informed the family, 'Shekhar has come down from the US. His father is looking for a suitable bride for him. But their demands are very high. If you are interested, I can try.'

'Please go ahead,' Gouramma responded promptly.

'No. We want to know what their expectations are. If we can afford it, only then will we want to go ahead,' intervened Shamanna.

'They want a good wedding along with a fully furnished apartment in Bangalore. It is not for the parents, but for the couple to stay in whenever they come from the US,' said the agent.

'That is beyond our capacity,' said Shamanna immediately, but Gouramma chose to overrule his objection.

'She is our only daughter. We will meet all their demands. Haven't we spent money on our sons' education? Just because Chandru and Jamuna are nice to us, we cannot rely on them entirely. It is Girish's duty also. Let him take a loan for his sister's marriage. If need be, we will also sell the house. I am not bothered.'

'Gouri, are we going to sell this, our own house, at this age, and live in a rented house? We should spend money only on what we can afford. Let us not get into any costly hassle.'

'I don't mind living in a rented house,' retorted Gouramma. 'But I want Surabhi to live in luxury in America.'

The argument went on. In the end, it was decided that Shekhar would come and meet Surabhi. Gouramma was a doting mother. In her eyes, Surabhi was a beauty, well read and accomplished. In actual fact, Surabhi was rather ordinary looking, read mostly stories in magazines and romantic novels and spent her time listening to film songs.

On the day Shekhar was to come and see Surabhi, Gouramma wanted elaborate snacks prepared for the evening visit. Vinuta was pregnant and had had a tiring day at school. Nevertheless, she did everything as per her mother-in-law's wishes, as the word 'no' did not exist in her dictionary.

The appointed time passed and Shekhar did not turn up.

Sudha Murty

'Perhaps he has to see three or four girls in a day and that is why they are late,' Girish commented.

Shekhar came, late in the evening, with his friends, glanced about the house and his expression changed. Girish noticed the look of disdain on his face. When he saw Surabhi, he was openly disappointed. His discomfort showed.

Girish broke the uncomfortable silence. 'My brother Chandru is in Nashville. Where do you work?'

In a heavy American accent, Shekhar replied, 'Chicago.'

'How long have you been there?'

'Oh! Many years.'

'Where do you work?'

'Westinghouse. Any more questions?' he asked, rudely.

Girish was annoyed. He had only been trying to have a conversation. When Shekhar was ready to leave, Gouramma told him, 'If you could inform us of your decision early, it will be a great favour. My daughter-in-law Jamuna wants to come for the wedding. Her father is Hosur Krishnappa.'

Shekhar just said, 'Yeah,' and went away.

Barely had Shekhar left when Gouramma stormed at Girish. 'Why did you have to ask him so many questions and make him uncomfortable? They might say no because of your rude behaviour.'

'Amma, my sister may get married to this man. Shouldn't we at least know this much about him, that too when he is staying in a far and unknown land?'

'Girish is absolutely right,' Shamanna opined.

'I am sure they will say yes. What did you think of that boy, Surabhi?'

'He looked a little old.' Surabhi grinned.

'Nothing of that sort! The difference is only eight years and that is okay. The other factors are very good. I must ask Jamuna and take her opinion. She will know everything.'

Vinuta remained silent. As usual, nobody had asked for her opinion. If there is no respect for the opinion of a particular member in a family, she thought bitterly, that person is an outsider.

Girish called out to her, 'Come, Vinu. Let's go for a stroll and get some vegetables. I am tired of sitting at home.'

'Vinu, you may be tired, particularly waiting on these people. Go and rest for a while,' said Shamanna. Vinu said she was all right, and went out with her husband.

'Vinu, I am really uncomfortable about Shekhar. I feel quite worried. I wish we knew someone in Chicago who could help us get some details.'

'The other day Madan came to visit your father. He said that he was based in Chicago. Why don't we ask him?'

Girish dropped the idea of buying vegetables and both of them walked to Madan's house. Fortunately, Madan and his old father were sitting and chatting in the veranda. There was no one else at home. Girish explained about Shekhar.

'Madan, please give us your frank opinion. How is the boy?'

His father responded immediately. 'The boy is very good. My niece was seen by him but there was some bad omen at our house so we did not pursue the matter.'

Madan did not say anything then. Only when he came up to the gate to see them off, did he hesitantly say, 'Girish, my father is old fashioned. He believes that one should not speak anything negative about others and that too particularly when discussing marriage. I don't believe in such things. I will tell you the facts and you can decide. But don't drag me into anything.'

'Of course not. Please tell us what you know.'

'I live in Chicago and so does Shekhar. Both of us are from Bangalore. Yet we never visited each other; we live fifty miles apart. One Sunday I suddenly decided to visit him as I was going to pass by that way. I did not call before dropping in. Shekhar was not at home. But I saw a white woman and I learnt that they were living-in. That is the reason we called off my cousin's proposal with him.'

Girish and Vinuta felt as if a very heavy weight had been taken off their shoulders.

'We are very grateful to you. You have saved my sister's life,' said Girish. They thanked their stars and silently walked back home.

That night, while having dinner, Gouramma started on her favourite topic. 'If Shekhar says yes, then which marriage hall shall we book? How many saris do we buy? How much gold and silver has to be given?' Nobody answered her, but she continued in the same vein. Finally Girish got fed up and said bluntly, 'Even if Shekhar agrees, we must turn it down.'

'What?' snapped Gouramma.

'I made some enquiries and learned that he has a live-in white girlfriend.'

'What rubbish! This is just a story made up by the people who can't bear our happiness and are jealous of us.'

'No. This was told to me by a well-wisher.' Then he explained what had happened.

Just then Girish heard a friend calling him from outside. He stood up and said sharply, 'Look, I have given my opinion. Despite that if you want to go ahead, you can,' and walked away.

Surabhi burst out crying as though the wedding had already been fixed and then called off.

Vinuta tried to comfort Surabhi. 'Surabhi, control yourself. It is good that I took your brother to Madan's house, otherwise we would not have known anything. You will definitely get a better husband. Shekhar is not worth crying for.'

Vinuta's wise words boomeranged on her. Tormented by feelings of defeat, despair and indignity, with the Gopi incident in the back of her mind, Gouramma burst out at poor Vinuta, pouring all the anger she felt towards Girish on her daughter-in-law. She blatantly disregarded the fact that she should be gentle since Vinu was pregnant. 'You are the one who incites Girish in this way. Otherwise, that stupid boy would not have behaved in this manner. Ever since you have come to this house, you are trying to keep him under your thumb. You saved the money in your marriage by not selling your house and made us hang our heads in shame. You are the siren who bewitches my son in a wrong direction.'

Stunned, Vinuta whispered, 'What are you saying?'

'What Amma is saying is nothing but the truth,' screeched Surabhi. 'You are jealous of me. Ever since you have come, I have noticed that you create a fight between Amma and Girish. You are doing everything possible to stop me from going to America. You want that I should live like you, earn my living by hard work and count every paisa. Learn from Jamuna. She is so generous and caring. You think if I become richer than you, then what will happen to you. You are also afraid that if this house has to be sold for my marriage, then you will become homeless and face difficulties. You are selfish to the core. Those are your real intentions and to hide them you play this stupid drama thinking you can fool everybody with your innocent smile. But you can't fool me. I understand everything.'

Shamanna, who had been listening to this tirade, lost his temper. 'Surabhi, hold your tongue!' he shouted.

'Appa, you are too gullible. Not all that glitters is gold. She is a very cunning woman. That is the reason people say you should bring brides from good families. Look at Jamuna! It reflects on her family. She is so unselfish and kind.'

'Surabhi! Your tongue is wagging too much. Let me pull it out before you say the next ugly word!' In a towering rage, Shamanna got up and even raised his hand to slap his daughter.

Shamanna had always been a kind teacher and had never used a stick at home or at school. He normally disliked harsh words and confrontations. Vinuta, who was standing next to him, caught hold of his hand just in time.

Vinuta realized that a particularly nasty storm was brewing in their house and that it could easily spiral into something worse. Surabhi had said something awful and she found it difficult to accept. Even in her worst nightmares, she had never thought that such terrible aspersions would be cast on her. Shocked, and badly hurt by the virulent attack, she knew that she had to try to control this fire. Tears poured down her cheeks and she did not try to wipe them. Letting her torment mix with the rice on her plate on the table, she told Surabhi, 'I have always thought of you as my sister and have wished for your happiness. That was why I took an interest in your marriage and tried my best to ensure your welfare. Now, I know my position, where I stand in your eyes. I will not meddle with anything concerning this family hereafter. Please forgive me.'

Leaving her meal unfinished, she rose from the table. Helpless, Shamanna just stood, dismayed at the terrible turn of events. Gouramma and Surabhi stayed immersed in their thoughts, avoiding Vinuta's pinched, wet face and continued to eat.

This was the first major conflict in their house, and the Dollar had played its insidious, evil part.

Ultimately, Surabhi got engaged to Suresh, a lawyer from Hyderabad. He satisfied most of Gouramma's conditions, particularly the no-mother-in-law clause. Suresh owned farmland, a big house and a fancy car. The only flaw was that he did not live in America but otherwise everything was perfect.

Vinuta was only a silent onlooker through all the negotiations. The differences in the attitudes of her family and her in-laws had struck her all of a sudden. She had woken up to Gouramma's and Surabhi's selfish and mean nature, and had resigned herself to the inevitable.

Girish wasn't very communicative. And Gouramma was after all his mother. So he could not feel the intensity of the pain that Vinu was going through. As the days went by, Vinuta shrivelled up, like a flower closing its petals to protect its soft vulnerable core. But then, life had trained her to live in pain. She did not take long to adjust to the new atmosphere of oppression she felt in the house.

The other person who had really been hurt was Shamanna. The home that had been a cosy haven so far had suddenly erupted like an inferno, the flames of which were blistering its very soul. The demon Dollar had devoured its peace and harmony.

Surabhi's engagement was celebrated with great pomp. Jamuna sent two hundred dollars as a gift.

Shamanna's house now had a computer, and e-mail and chatting had brought down the phone bills. Chandru had sent an e-mail. 'This year, we are going to be short of holidays. Jamuna too is working in a bank now. Work out a convenient date for everybody and inform us early, so that we can plan for a two-week break to attend the wedding.'

Vinuta's baby was due in August. December was unacceptable to the groom's family.

Uncomfortable in the house now, Vinuta decided to go to Dharwad for her baby's delivery. 'That is my home town. I have a house there. My grandmother, Seetakka, will come over. There are good hospitals. I have decided that that is the best place for me to deliver my child.' It was probably the first time she had spoken her mind and put her foot down.

It was decided that July was convenient for all but Jamuna sent an e-mail. 'It is summer in Europe and we have planned a trip. We cannot cancel it. If I have to attend the wedding, then it has to be on a date convenient to me. I will also give some dollars. But if you want that Vinuta should attend the wedding, decide on a date suitable to her. I might not be able to come.' Things had come to a flashpoint: this was going to be a fight for power, to be decided by money. It was a tussle between the Dollar and the Rupee. Jamuna had bluntly made that clear.

Shamanna said, 'Gouri, Vinuta's delivery date cannot be changed. The best thing would be to fix a date in July so that Vinuta can attend the wedding and then go to Dharwad for her delivery. Jamuna can postpone her Europe trip to next year, or they can come for just one week to attend the wedding. Actually I would prefer their visit to be brief.'

But Gouramma had an entirely different viewpoint. She shook her head. 'No, that won't be right. How can we afford to upset Jamuna? We have to fix a date convenient to her. You should not meddle in such matters.'

Sudha Murty

Vinuta understood perfectly the hidden meaning of these statements. Chandru and Jamuna had contributed two and a half lakh for the wedding; Girish and Vinuta had managed just one lakh. So Gouramma's reasoning was: they who put in more, get to dictate terms. Gouramma was dancing to the tune of the Dollar Bahu.

So the wedding was fixed for a date in August. Vinuta had to move to Dharwad much before the wedding. Gouramma, swelling with 'status', told everyone, 'Jamuna, my elder daughter-in-law, is coming specifically for this wedding from America.'

Shamanna was concerned about Vinuta and her delivery. Gouramma too made a great show of concern. She told everyone that she had advised Vinuta to deliver the baby in Bangalore, but Vinuta had insisted on going to Dharwad. So, Gouramma said, she had decided to respect her feelings. Vinuta delivered a baby boy two weeks before Surabhi's wedding.

The wedding went off very well. Gouramma felt a renewed vigour and verve now that her precious son and Dollar Bahu were there. Jamuna, on her part, did not contribute in any way to the proceedings. She spent most of her time shopping, visiting her family, changing into different clothes for every occasion and posing in front of the cameras.

She had brought plenty of chiffon and georgette saris for Surabhi. That pleased Gouramma and she in turn showered gifts on her darling Dollar Bahu. Although Jamuna smiled for the cameras, in her heart of hearts she resented Gouramma lavishing needless expensive gifts on Surabhi. She had worked hard for the money, away from her homeland and under tough conditions, which was being so carelessly spent on the ceremonies and on gifts. She fumed at the way their money was being misused. Of course, she never showed it.

Why should I feel bitter? I shall just reduce the monthly allowance that we send. Then they will control their expenses on their own. It would be easy to justify, thought Jamuna.

To please Jamuna, Gouramma would say, 'But for Jamuna, we would not have hosted the wedding with such grandeur.' Never once did she even mention Girish; any mention of Vinuta was of course not to be expected.

Girish went to Dharwad to see his newborn son. Shamanna named him Harsha. Surabhi left with her husband. She did not even bother to call Vinuta and say goodbye. She was engrossed in her new life with her rich husband. Chandru planned to visit Dharwad, and Jamuna promptly went to her parents' house.

✧

Chandru was in Dharwad after eight long years. The last time he had been there, there had been much uncertainty in his life. How things had changed since then. His fellow passenger had become his sister-in-law. At that time he had dreamt of going to America, heaven on earth. Today, he acknowledged that it was a great country, and his geographical knowledge had increased. But more than anything else, he now understood one major truth: Ever since he had started earning in dollars, people respected him, envied him and showed him that extra bit of warmth. In the process, however, he had also lost real love and mutual trust. It was an unalterable fact that no amount of dollars could buy the warmth of genuine affection.

Chandru stayed in Hotel Dharwad. Dharwad had changed a lot. The population had increased and horse-drawn tongas on the roads had become rare: rickshaws had replaced them. Apartment blocks had replaced the vast lush green stretches of open space. Youngsters had migrated to bigger cities and Dharwad had become a city for the older generation.

Chandru went to Vinuta's house. The garden was the same but not quite as green and colourful as it had been when he had last seen it. That was natural, perhaps, since it did not have Vinu around to lavish care on it.

Vinuta was pleased to see Chandru. It was a pleasant surprise that he had come to see the baby. After the preliminary niceties, Vinuta asked about the wedding and enquired after Jamuna.

'The marriage went off very well. Jamuna is fine too. Can I take Harsha on my lap?'

The proud mother handed over her doll-like baby.

Chandru kept up a happy chatter, but suddenly thought of something. 'Vinuta, do you remember you often sang a song whose lyrics were something like, *In the lush green forest, the koel proves to sing/ Shunning in contempt all the powers of the king.*

Vinuta smiled nostalgically, 'Yes, of course I remember.'

'Do you still sing?'

'Chandru, the koel has understood her position. She has stopped singing,' Vinuta said in a sad tone.

'Why? Is she afraid of the powers of the king?'

'Where is the king? Where is the mango tree? The greed for money has killed the spirit of the koel.'

'No. Don't call it the greed for money,' said Chandru coolly. 'Greed for the Dollar would be more accurate.'

Vinuta stayed silent and Chandru understood her pain. He sighed. 'Vinuta, I am unhappy.'

'I can't believe that. You have everything in life. You are rich. You are in America. You have a wife like Jamuna. Your mother and sister dote on you . . .'

'You, Vinuta, are living among your own people, speaking the same language, sharing the same culture. Your child will grow up with his grandparents, with the same set of values. You are not compelled to live in another country with a different language and alien climatic conditions.'

'Chandru, the grass always looks greener on the other side.'

'Doesn't this hold true for you too?'

Vinuta still did not understand why Chandru was unhappy in the nirvana that was America.

'Vinuta, you have no idea of the life there. Just buying things, counting dollars, living in a big house, does not make everyone happy. They also have their own set of problems.'

'Jamuna does not say that. She always praises America!'

'Vinuta, we are in two different worlds, two different cultures. We are lonely.'

'Then why don't you come back?'

'I have grown used to that life. I know, if I come back I have to forgo many things, something that I am not ready to do just yet . . . Forget about me for the moment, tell me about you.'

'To be honest with you, I am not at all that happy either. All the time, there is comparison between Jamuna and me. I don't want and can't compete with anybody. But it is evident that the family does not need me any more. I'm sorry, but that's the truth,' Vinuta confided in Chandru, finding him more a friend than a brother-in-law, in Dharwad.

Chandru had to leave soon after. He went away with a heavy heart.

Vinuta returned to Bangalore with her six-month-old son and he became Shamanna's darling. When Vinuta was at school, Shamanna would gladly babysit, showering the child with care and affection.

Surabhi was very happy in Hyderabad. Vinuta noticed that, of late, Jamuna's parents never visited them at all.

One day, Gouramma was grinding batter for dosas when she felt a sharp pain in her chest. She ignored the pain but the next day, while having her bath, she felt a lump in her breast. She thought if she just washed it with warm water, it would break, and she shrugged it off. When the lump did not go away after a week, she began to worry.

She called Vinuta who was getting ready to go to school and showed her the lump. Vinuta promptly applied for leave and took Gouramma to the doctor. She did not talk of this either with Shamanna or with Girish. She was scared, but kept calm. She behaved as if everything was normal.

After examining the patient, the doctor called Vinuta aside and asked what her relationship was with the patient. 'She is my mother-in-law. Is there any problem?'

'There is a lump-like growth in her breast. We will have to do a biopsy and only after that can we reach any diagnosis.'

'What does that mean? Is it dangerous in any way?'

'I really cannot say anything at this point. Let us carry out the biopsy first.'

Vinuta came out and Gouramma asked her, 'What cream has he given? How soon will it clear?'

'You will soon be all right it seems.'

Back home, Vinuta sat in quiet thought.

Chandru was far away and there was no point in worrying him. If Surabhi was informed, she would surely blow it all out of proportion. Shamanna was already old and should not be burdened with fresh worries. She decided to tell Girish everything that night.

With tears in his eyes, Girish asked the question which had been uppermost in Vinuta's mind all day. 'Do you think Amma has cancer?'

'Why should we assume the worst? Let's wait for the biopsy report.'

The next day Vinuta took another day's leave from school and took Gouramma to the hospital for the exploratory operation. Gouramma was scared at the very word 'operation' and kept saying, 'Don't inform Surabhi or Jamuna. They will be worried. They may drop all their work and rush here.' Vinuta never responded.

After the operation, Gouramma had to stay in hospital for a day. As she was in the women's ward, Vinuta stayed with her.

The patient in the neighbouring bed asked Gouramma, 'Is she your daughter?' Gouramma answered, in all her arrogance, 'My daughter stays in Hyderabad and my elder daughter-in-law is in America. This is my younger daughter-in-law.'

The reports showed that the growth in Gouramma's breast was benign. Girish was relieved. He sent an e-mail to his brother.

That week, Girish's bank colleagues had planned a family holiday to Karwar and Gokarna. Vinuta said, 'Amma is alone and scared. She requires company. I shall stay back.'

'Jamuna is coming next month for her brother's wedding. If you inform her of my condition, she will come immediately and look after me. You can go on the tour,' said Gouramma shamelessly.

Shamanna was embarrassed by his wife's behaviour. In spite of Vinuta's dutiful caring, Gouramma never acknowledged Vinuta.

On learning the news, Surabhi phoned and talked to her mother. She did not bother to visit though.

Chandru sent a cheque for three hundred dollars to cover the expenses and replied to Girish's mail: 'Anyone can help in the form of money. But one should not forget the presence and care of people around you. Amma, you are very lucky that you have someone who looks after you so well.'

For Gouramma, these comments were like water off a duck's back. The cheque meant more; it was, in fact, everything.

Chandru came to Bangalore on a business visit. Surabhi and Suresh came from Hyderabad to meet him. Jamuna was pregnant. Gouramma was more concerned about the unborn baby than the grandchild growing up in front of her eyes.

'How is Jamuna? What is the due date? Does she like pickles or sweets? Does she have nausea? Has she put on weight?' She harried Chandru with a string of queries.

Harsha had begun to walk and would run around the house. He was healthy and as sweet as his mother. Shamanna spent all his time looking after his grandson. Vinuta, on her part, had become thin and frail like a drooping flower. She looked depressed and went about the housework in a listless, machine-like manner.

There was no communication any more between Gouramma and Vinuta, other than instructions concerning household chores. The initial bridge of affection and trust seemed to have rusted.

Chandru had brought a lot of toys for Harsha but Vinuta pointed out, 'You should not be spending so much money on Harsha. We cannot afford such expensive gifts in return.' Chandru was stunned that Vinuta would make a comment like this. She was the one person he knew who had never bothered about status or money.

'Vinuta, Harsha is the first grandchild of our family and he will always get the best,' said Chandru, hoping that would put the matter to rest.

Gouramma's long-standing dream was about to come true. She had been expressing, for some time now, her wish to visit America in order to take care of her Dollar Bahu during her pregnancy and after the delivery. But Shamanna was equally insistent on not going. 'I can't stay away from Harsha for such a long time. You can go, and take your time to come back.'

So it was decided that Gouramma would go to America on her own. She began her preparations. She would call Jamuna regularly to ask what she could bring. The atmosphere in the house became even more America centric. Everyone secretly awaited Gouramma's departure.

Gouramma prayed in different temples for the well-being and safe delivery of her Dollar Bahu's baby. Surabhi bought an expensive sari for her dear sister-in-law. Gouramma also prepared lots of delicious eatables, masala powders, chutneys and pickles, which she packed in a separate bag.

'Amma, please remember that you also have a son here. You can probably open a shop with the quantity and varieties you have prepared. How about leaving some for us?' the normally docile Girish joked.

'Girish, you are in India. You can go out and eat in any restaurant. Poor Jamuna, where can she go?'

Vinuta watched in silence. She remembered how they had treated her when she was pregnant: no gifts, no sweets, not even a tender word. 'If you want to buy anything or eat anything, you can go and eat outside with Girish,' was what she had been told. When Harsha was born, Gouramma had sent one hundred rupees on the occasion of his naming ceremony. Vinuta felt all this was so unfair, especially when she had always done whatever Gouramma expected of her. But she said nothing.

Jamuna's mother too sent plenty of gifts for her daughter. Immediately, Gouramma was worried. 'I have bought a gold chain for the baby and a silk sari for Jamuna. Do you think it is enough? Our gifts should not look small in front of what her parents have given.'

The normally calm Shamanna lost his temper. 'Go and stay with your son for a good five years. Thousands of people go abroad to help with their children's deliveries. You behave as if your daughter-in-law is the only one in the world who is pregnant . . . The day you board the flight, I shall have my first night of peaceful sleep in years!'

'You have never taken me anywhere,' Gouramma shot back. 'It is my good fortune that I have a son and a daughter-in-law like Chandru and Jamuna. They have called me to the US with such affection. You people are just jealous.'

That night, Surabhi and Gouramma had a whispered conference. 'Amma, I have convinced Suresh that he must go abroad and take up a job. I don't want to stay home and look after my father-in-law. It will be fun to live abroad. But Suresh says he has to take up the bar exam there.'

'It is an excellent idea,' Gouramma said enthusiastically. 'Anyway, I will be there for a year. You can both come and stay with Jamuna. Suresh can prepare for his exams and I am sure he will get through.'

'It is not just that, Amma. Travel will cost a lot of money, and we will need to live in their house for a year.'

With complete confidence Gouramma said, 'Of course Jamuna will take care of that. She is very generous. She loves you and she will obey me. Start your preparations.'

Surabhi returned to Hyderabad, duly reassured.

The following day, when Shamanna heard of this plan, he was most upset. 'Once the children are married, we should not interfere in their lives. They are all grown up. Staying in somebody's house for a year! Chandru may not like it, and we do not know the situation there.'

'I know my son and daughter-in-law very well. They will definitely do it for Surabhi,' Gouramma retorted.

Chandru's friend Ashwat and his wife, a Kannada-speaking couple from Bangalore, were to fly to Nashville and Chandru arranged for his mother to fly with them. He also sent the plane ticket, along with a letter about the things that she could or couldn't carry on the plane and other bits of advice.

Gouramma did not enjoy the flight. She felt uncomfortable with the seat belt on. She found it difficult to use the toilet. She was a vegetarian and did not like the food she was served. Besides, she could not eat unless she had had a bath. And she was nervous. But all those troubles vanished when the plane touched down at Nashville airport, and when she walked out and saw Chandru waiting for her. Emotion choked her as soon as she saw her beloved son in this wonderful country. She was unable to speak.

It was a small airport and Chandru collected the luggage and put it in the boot of the car. Gouramma took one look at the splendid car and puffed with pride. 'Jamuna had sent a picture of the car to us. Is it the same one?'

'Yes, Amma.'

'Why did she not come to receive me?'

'She had to go to office. She will be back before we reach home.'

'How can she be working in this advanced stage of pregnancy?'

'Here women work till the last day . . .'

Gouramma happily sat back in the comfortable car to enjoy the drive. Chandru leaned over to fasten her seat belt, but she protested, 'I am not a small child that I am going to fall off my seat. Remove this belt.'

'No, Amma. It is the law in this country.'

As a matter of routine, Gouramma had expected Jamuna to come to the airport and welcome her respectfully. Hadn't she herself gone to drop and pick up Jamuna at Bangalore airport, every time? Even Jamuna's mother had not bothered on a few occasions.

This was the first shock, but in the excitement of seeing America for the first time, Gouramma mentally pardoned Jamuna. She caught glimpses of the scenery, the wide roads, the high-speed cars, and was amazed. Though it was cold outside, it was quite warm in the car. There was a fascinating variety of trees on both sides of the road. There was hardly anyone walking on the road though. She sighed and thought to herself, this is America. What a difference between this land and India. No teeming crowds or cyclists pushing their way through, no rickshaws, cows, bulls, donkeys, horses, hand-carts; just zooming cars and more cars. The Hindu epics describe different kinds of worlds like *nagaloka, yakshaloka, kinnaraloka.* What kind of *loka* is this?

Chandru spoke, and she switched off thoughts of the unnamed *loka.* 'How is everyone at home? How is Harsha?'

'Oh, he has grown up to be very naughty. When I was about to leave, he held on to my pallu and insisted that he wanted to come along. But when he was told that his grandfather was not going, he promptly let go. They are very attached to each other.'

'Harsha is so lucky. He is enjoying the love of both grandparents. I wish Appa had come. It would have been wonderful.'

'You know your father. He is not interested in anything. He could have seen this great country with his own eyes. Instead, he has chosen to stay back. Thank God he allowed me to come! Never mind that now. Tell me, how is Jamuna? When is she due?'

'She is due in another fifteen days. We are going to have a baby girl. We have decided to name her Manasi.'

Gouramma was surprised. Everything had been decided before the delivery. Back in India, no preparations were made before the birth of the child.

Soon Chandru stopped the car in front of a large bungalow with a huge front lawn. A cement road ran through it, apparently for cars. What sort of office is this? wondered Gouramma.

Chandru said, 'Come on, Amma. We are home.'

'This is your house, Chandru? This mansion?' Gouramma's eyes were wide with wonder. Imagine that small house in Jayanagar! How could you compare it with this one, she thought.

When Gouramma walked up to the front door, she could not believe that the woman who opened the door was indeed her darling Jamuna. Where was the Jamuna whom she had last seen at Surabhi's wedding, in a silk sari, decked in gold and gem-studded ornaments? This Jamuna looked so bare. She looked so strange with her short hair, a loose gown, and neither a bindi nor her mangalsutra! The only improvement was that her complexion had brightened.

Jamuna smiled. 'How are you, Amma? How was the journey?'

Sudha Murty

'It was fine,' Gouramma replied crisply and stepped into the house. She had expected that Jamuna would welcome her by touching her feet, neatly dressed in a sari, wearing gold and diamond jewellery. She had carefully composed and rehearsed her blessing. But she was disappointed.

Gouramma stood for a minute in confusion. Jamuna guessed what was going on in Gouramma's mind and just walked into the house without letting on. Gouramma silently followed her to the formal drawing room and in sheer relief of reaching home, sat on the sofa, relaxing a bit, observing the opulence around her.

It was a rich man's house, with plush carpets, beautiful curtains, a big television, a lovely rosewood dining table with silverware on it, sandalwood artefacts. There was a fabulous chandelier too. This house was even more spectacular than Krishnappa's farmhouse.

'Amma, will you have coffee now?' asked Jamuna.

'I don't eat or drink until I have had a bath. Show me the bathroom.'

Jamuna took her to the bathroom. Gouramma was shocked to see the commode and the bathtub in the same room.

'There is a toilet in the bathroom. How can I have bath here and perform the puja? Show me a separate bath.'

Jamuna looked at Chandru, leaving it to him to explain to his mother. 'Amma, this is not like India. You should not expect everything to be as it is there. In our house, all the bedrooms have an attached bath-cum-toilet like this. While you have a bath, pull the curtain so that you do not have to see the toilet.'

'Chandru, I am scared of using the tub. Get me a bucket. I will put it in the tub and have a bath. I am not used to these hand showers.'

Chandru sighed. 'Amma, next time I go to an Indian store, I will get you a bucket. But for now, I shall bring you a big vessel.'

After an unsatisfactory bath, Gouramma dressed and came out. The room appears a little dark, she thought, and it was indeed pitch dark outside, but the clock showed it was just four in the afternoon.

Gouramma was mystified. 'Chandru, how come it is already dark? It's not even five o'clock.'

'It's winter, Amma. It gets dark here quite early.'

After she had finished her coffee, Chandru took her on a tour of the house. 'Our house is a little ordinary compared to other houses here. There are houses with seven bedrooms and four car parks.' Gouramma's room, like all the others, had a fluffy carpet. Even the mattress was soft. All the curtains were pretty and everything matched . . . and Chandru called this an ordinary house! Gouramma was confused.

'Chandru, don't be so modest. Your house is like a palace.'

'No, Amma. You have not seen other houses. I remember Appa telling me of a fable in Sanskrit. It seems in the Malaya mountains the women burnt precious sandalwood as kindling. Similarly in this country, these are all very ordinary things.'

Jamuna took her to the kitchen. It was so clean that Gouramma felt that nobody had ever cooked there. It was a modern kitchen with all the latest hi-tech electrical gadgets.

'How long are you still going to work, Jamuna?'

'Only this week. Then I want to stay home and relish the taste of your cooking. When the baby is two months old, I shall go back to work.'

'Jamuna, do you need to work when the baby is still so small? I understand that Vinuta has to work because Girish has an ordinary job. You are like a queen here. You have two cars.'

Jamuna did not reply. 'Amma, everyone has to carry his own weight here. We buy the house, car and furniture on instalments and so every month we have to pay back some of that loan. That's why Jamuna has to work. Anyway, she would get bored at home.' Chandru effectively closed the conversation.

Gouramma was amazed to hear that even here it was a matter of loans and instalments. She liked the idea, but only the first part—that anybody could buy anything.

The next day, Chandru and Jamuna went to work and Gouramma stayed alone in that spacious house. She was still feeling jet-lagged. While she was lying on the bed, she remembered her promise to Surabhi. She reasoned, Chandru has such a big house. A couple staying in one room in a corner will not affect anyone. Surabhi will look after the baby and Jamuna can work as usual.

She remembered how she had stayed with her brother's family for two years when Shamanna had been transferred to some godforsaken village. She had always felt that it was the right of a sister to stay in her brother's house. She applied the same logic for Surabhi. If Surabhi comes here, she too will settle down here and then two of my children will be NRIs over a period of time. I can visit them any time, she thought to herself dreamily. How could a woman, educated only up to the fourth standard, understand the complexity of the modern world?

A week after her arrival Chandru took Gouramma to the department store. It was so huge and clean, everything arranged neatly on shelves. Gouramma was fascinated with the varieties of fresh fruit juices stored in cans, in boxes, in so many different sizes. And the flavours of ice creams! Everything was available under one roof. Even though Gouramma had seen departmental stores in Bangalore, they were nothing in comparison to this one.

In a short time Gouramma learnt to use the microwave, the toaster, the electric kettle and the cooking range. The only chore she hated was cleaning the dishes, something she had never done even in her own house. They had always had a maid for that job. But in America, one did not get domestic help, she realized, so she had to learn to handle the dishwasher and washing machine.

As was the custom in India, Gouramma wanted to perform the ritual of giving the mother-to-be all her favourite food and special gifts, to keep her happy and cheerful during the last few days of her pregnancy. So Gouramma had brought with her the traditional green sari and specially prepared sweetmeats for the occasion.

She told Jamuna, 'This Friday is an auspicious day. Invite a few women, whomever you want. We can have the ceremony and "aarti". I will cook a great meal. We will lay all the eatables, gifts, flowers and things on a side table. We can have a special table to display the gifts given by the guests.'

Jamuna at once dismissed her suggestion. 'Amma, nobody will come for such programmes on a working day. We will invite everyone after the delivery.'

Gouramma wanted to show off how good a mother-in-law she was, but Jamuna did not give her the chance. Helpless, she was forced to give her gift without performing the ceremony. She noticed that Jamuna did not even bother to open the gift. A couple of days later, when Jamuna went into labour, Gouramma immediately offered to go with her to the hospital. Chandru said, 'Amma, you stay at home. That's more practical. I will go with her into the delivery room. I have taken lessons. I will inform you once the baby is delivered.' He did not give her a chance to talk, and left with Jamuna, who was by then groaning in pain.

Gouramma sat down, anxiously, near the telephone and started praying for a safe delivery. She did not understand why a man was allowed in the delivery room when there was a woman around to help. After what seemed a very long time, Chandru called up to say, 'Jamuna has safely delivered a baby girl and she will be back tomorrow. You need not come to the hospital.'

Gouramma was happy, but horrified that the mother was coming back within a day. But there was nobody to whom she could voice her concerns.

When Jamuna came home, Gouramma saw the baby was thin and rather plain-looking, like her mother. A separate room for the newborn had been prepared much in advance with a special cradle, colourful curtains and lots of toys. Tucking the baby into the cradle, Jamuna headed towards her room. At this, Gouramma could just not keep quiet. 'How can such a small baby sleep alone?' she snapped. 'If you want, I can sleep with her.'

'No. Please don't do that. Manasi should get used to sleeping alone in her room. That's how it is here.' Without giving her mother-in-law a chance to say anything more, Jamuna sailed away to her bedroom and shut the door.

Gouramma was stunned by her rudeness!

She remembered Harsha. He slept with his grandparents. That could be the reason why he was inseparable from his grandfather. How could these people expect a bond to develop between parents and children when they brought up their children amidst loneliness? Gouramma was worried.

The next day Jamuna was bathing the baby in a tub and Gouramma pleaded, 'Let me massage and bathe the baby. Get me some baby oil. I will do it. Infants should get plenty of sleep and a good bath for proper growth.'

'No. I don't like that sort of thing. It's all right in India. Here the bathing tub will become oily. Everyone will laugh at us. I shall follow the childcare book to raise my baby.'

Gouramma had never studied any book to learn how to raise a child. And in her neighbourhood she was famous for the wonderful baths she gave newborn babies. Many new mothers would request her to bathe their babies and Gouramma willingly helped. She did it out of love and not as a profession. When those children grew up and passed their examinations, they would come and take her blessings. Their proud mothers would say, 'You had bathed him in his infancy. He is an officer now.' Gouramma would beam with pride and joy on such occasions.

She suddenly remembered Harsha and Vinuta. Vinuta was good at all the household work but when it came to bathing the baby, she always wanted Gouramma to do it. Who is giving Harsha a bath now that she was not there, she worried.

J amuna's two months' maternity leave was about to end
and she decided to invite a few of her special friends for
a naming ceremony on a Sunday. Gouramma was very
enthusiastic since she loved cooking and feeding people.
This was a great chance for her to show off her culinary
skills. She started preparing three days in advance.

Since it was a Sunday most Indian men and women,
irrespective of which part of the country they came from
or what their mother tongue was, were able to attend. The
common language in this crowd was English. Everyone
brought gifts, things that were useful for the baby, which
were displayed on the table. Gouramma also gave her gifts
but no one seemed to appreciate them. The ceremony was
not a religious one, as it would have been in Bangalore,
and was over in no time. But the party went on till late in
the evening.

All the guests left, except one, and Chandru hurried to
clean up the basement, which was in quite a clutter after
the lunch. Claiming she was tired Jamuna put the baby in
its room, and settled down to chat with her friend Rekha.
Gouramma, too, needed rest but no one told her to take it
easy. So she went into the kitchen to clean up the mess.

Rekha was praising the food. 'Today's food was great.
Jamuna, have one more baby while your mother-in-law is
still here and complete the family.'

'Are you kidding? We can't afford a second baby. You
know how expensive it is to bring up even one child! We

are ordinary people and like everyone, we too have plenty of mortgages to clear. Besides, I prefer a small family.'

'Why do you say that?' said Rekha.

'In my family we are just two siblings. My mother never liked big crowds encroaching on our privacy. The best way to meet relatives is at functions. Don't invite anyone to come and stay in your house, she always says.'

'You are right, Jamuna. Last month, my brother-in-law came from India for some work and stayed with us for one full month. I was really stressed. We have our own lifestyles. When an outsider comes, I feel we have to work extra. Freezing the food for a week and warming it up before eating is normal for us. But they find it odd. I do not know what my brother-in-law must have said back at home about me. He may have complained that I gave him stale food.'

'You are absolutely right, Rekha. It is better to send some money for a gift than to have someone stay in your house.' Jamuna looked around and said in a hushed voice, 'In a way I am lucky. My brother-in-law and his wife will never be able to afford to come here, though my sister-in-law is greedy. But they cannot come here because her husband is only a lawyer. Even if they want to come, I can put them off on some pretext.'

Though Jamuna was whispering, Gouramma heard everything, and she could not sleep the whole night. She had always assumed that there would be a red carpet laid out for Surabhi. She noticed that Chandru always obeyed his wife, which was not the case with Girish. If Jamuna said no to something, there was no way Chandru could go against her wishes.

Gouramma could understand Chandru's behaviour. In a far-off place, away from family, a husband and wife have only each other to depend on, they have nobody else to turn to. Hence they tended to stick together. In India, when sons fought with their wives, some mothers-in-law were happy, and added fuel to the fire by taking their sons' side. Such mothers-in-law would never try to support the daughter-in-law. But in this country, such situations just would not arise.

Chandru had become immensely successful at work but his personality had changed. He had become subdued, always immersed in thought. Jamuna, on the other hand, had become more outgoing, perhaps because she had more freedom and because of her job which involved meeting people and exchanging ideas with them. She had an opinion on every matter and argued over every small thing and always won. She was the boss of the family.

One day Gouramma asked Chandru what he pondered over all the time, and he explained, 'Amma, I have a friend called Venkat. He is from Karnataka and he has a thirteen-year-old daughter. She is going through the typical teenage problems. If her father asks where she goes and what she does, she throws tantrums.'

Gouramma said innocently, 'He should keep her in control by punishing her.'

'Amma, in this country you cannot "punish" children. They will call the police. Being Indians, we do not like our children to be like American children. When they are young, they mingle with other kids, talk in their accent and we feel very proud. But when they behave like American teenagers, we get upset. At times, I think about my daughter and get scared.'

'Why worry about it right now? We shall see about it after fifteen years. Now let us get ready to go out.' Jamuna hurriedly changed the topic, but for the first time, Gouramma understood what was bothering Chandru.

Jamuna prepared to resume work. She taught Gouramma how to feed the baby with the bottle. Gouramma pleaded, 'Jamuna, such small babies need mother's milk. Vinuta would come home every afternoon to feed Harsha.'

Jamuna shrugged it off. 'I will pump my breast milk and keep it in the fridge. You can warm it and give it to the baby at the right time. And by the way, I do not want to follow Vinuta's example in everything. This is America.'

When Jamuna and Chandru left for work, the house became really quiet. Gouramma was not a talkative person, but somehow she never liked being alone for long periods. Manasi was a good baby and she slept for long stretches. Gouramma did not know how to kill time.

Initially she enjoyed the outings to the supermarkets, picnics, drives. But soon they became monotonous. She started missing her life in Bangalore and her own home. In Bangalore she could go wherever she wanted and never needed to depend on anybody. Vinuta and Shamanna looked after the house. She was a member of a women's club in the nearby temple and most evenings all her friends would meet up and start their gossip sessions. By the time Gouramma finished her stories and came home, dinner would be waiting for her. She did not have to worry about any particular responsibilities in the house.

Here, she did not have any friends at all. She knew only Kannada; she could not converse in English. And over the weekends, Chandru and Jamuna were always busy with housework—cleaning the car, cleaning the driveway, vacuuming the house and other household chores.

Gouramma enjoyed serving guests her special dishes, but nobody came visiting or dropped in here. In Bangalore, she could invite any number of people for meals, but here, she had to take Jamuna's permission. She would often pray that someone should drop in on the weekends. But visiting someone meant travelling at least forty miles. Initially she had enjoyed going out, but now she didn't enjoy the long drives.

One day, Chandru hesitantly asked, 'Amma, my friend Radhakrishna, his wife Savitri and their daughter Savita would like to come and spend some time with us. Is it okay with you and Jamuna?'

Immediately Jamuna replied, 'There will be so much of cooking to do. Amma will get tired. Anyway, they are so rich, why can't they stay in a hotel?'

'No, Jamuna. They want to stay with us. When I was a bachelor in Florida, I have stayed in their house many times, and they took good care of me. I cannot ask them to stay in a hotel.'

For the first time Gouramma opposed her daughter-in-law. 'Let them come, Chandru. I will handle all the kitchen work, without bothering anybody. I hope they can speak Kannada.' In her heart, she was outraged by Jamuna's attitude. She felt that although this house was big, it had a small heart. If Vinuta had ever said such a thing, Gouramma would have scolded her until she was forced to apologize. But Gouramma did not dare speak her mind to Jamuna. She was, after all, the Dollar Bahu.

twenty

Gouramma was eagerly looking forward to the arrival of Radhakrishna and his family. Since vegetables, fruits and groceries are not too highly priced in America, she thought to herself, I will make lots of dishes for the guests, savouries and sweets. And since they speak Kannada, it will be a refreshing change to have a conversation with outsiders.

Jamuna was of course highly upset at this turn of events. Gouramma had spoilt her plans. If her mother-in-law had not been there, Jamuna would have somehow managed to put the guests off. As Gouramma had taken Chandru's side, he had become stronger, she felt. She considered it a personal insult. For the first time she faced a situation in which her wish had not counted in her own home.

Radhakrishna was a very senior scientist in a reputed company and had earned a good name and fortune. His wife Savitri was a traditional lady, in her early fifties. As soon as they arrived, she bowed down and touched Gouramma's feet. Gouramma was delighted with this gesture.

Chandru and Radhakrishna caught up as they sipped their filter coffee and munched on the Indian snacks that Gouramma had prepared. Jamuna made a great show of courtesy, and politely told Savitri, 'I am going to my friend Rekha's house to pick up some Kannada DVDs that she has got from India. You can all enjoy the movies.'

She left the baby at home and Savita played with Manasi. Gouramma began cooking and Savitri joined her to help. Gouramma felt uncomfortable having a guest working in the kitchen. But Savitri reassured her, 'Amma, this is America where we do not have servants. When we go to somebody's house, we cannot behave like guests and sit outside. Please don't say no. It will be too much work for you.' Efficiently, she cut the vegetables as she chatted with Gouramma. Gouramma noticed a slight pall of grief around the couple.

Jamuna returned home at lunchtime.

In the evening, Gouramma got ready to take Manasi for a stroll in her pram. This was her routine every day, and Savitri decided to join her. After a while, Gouramma casually asked, 'Is Savita your only child?' Savitri burst into tears. Gouramma hastily apologized, 'Oh, I am so sorry! I do not know anything. Have I hurt you?'

Wiping her tears, Savitri said, 'No. That is a perfectly normal question. But my mind is so full of grief that I burst into tears easily.'

'What is the matter?' Gouramma asked sympathetically.

'Don't even ask! What has not happened to us! We came to America eighteen years ago and now, this has become our country. When we came here, our first daughter Shama was five years old. We were very particular that Shama respect our traditions and culture, and not become like American girls. So we celebrated every festival at home and made it a point to attend most of the Indian community gatherings. We would also invite our Indian friends very often. We sent her every year to my mother's place in India to absorb our culture. We would always tell her that though we were the citizens of America we were Indians.'

Gouramma could not see where all this was leading. Savitri continued, 'We came from a small town in Karnataka and from an extremely orthodox family. When Shama turned twenty-one, while she was still a student, we decided to get her married.'

'That's very strange. When a girl is studying, even in India, we don't get her married nowadays,' said Gouramma.

'We were afraid that she would get into wrong company and find a boyfriend or some such thing, so we decided to get her married. We advertised in the papers in India for a groom. The response was amazing. Most of them were very good, and at last Shama liked Surendra. He came from a middle-class family and was very intelligent. We never suspected anything amiss. We celebrated the wedding on a lavish scale, spending an enormous amount of money. We gave good gifts to all the guests from both sides. Surendra came to the US along with us and we gifted them an apartment. He wanted to study further, and we paid his tuition fee too. Life was smooth for some time.'

Once again, Savitri began to cry. Gouramma stopped walking and thinking something had happened to Surendra, tried to comfort Savitri, 'It is all god's will.' Instantly Savitri stopped crying and snapped, 'There was no god involved in this. Once Surendra got his scholarship, his whole attitude towards Shama changed completely. Every day they had massive fights. He would repeatedly tell her, "I just married you out of sympathy. Go and look at your face." Actually, he had married her only because she was an American citizen. Eventually, they got a divorce.'

'Where are they now?'

'Surendra completed his studies, went back to India, and married again. In India, nobody bothered to find out why the divorce had taken place. And Surendra could fabricate stories about our daughter which nobody could verify. But the damage was more to Shama. After the divorce, she took out all her anger on us. "You have destroyed my life. I am sick of your Indian arranged marriage system. Without knowing anything about me, he married me only for the chance to come here. From now on I want to live the way I want. Don't you dare interfere!'" she told us.'

'So where is she now?'

'She doesn't communicate very regularly. She calls us up once in a while. She is pursuing her studies in California and lives with a Brazilian boyfriend. She rejected the money that we sent her. She works as a waitress in a restaurant in her free time.'

'What will happen to her?' Gouramma was worried.

'God only knows. Sometimes I shudder to think of her future. I come from a family of Vedic scholars, highly respected for their knowledge of our religion, philosophy, traditions and customs. And now, look at the irony! Our daughter is living with a Brazilian boy. What a shame to us! Where did we go wrong?'

Gouramma was horrified and baffled. How could a young girl do such things? She had seen many instances in her life where men had been nasty to women but the women had adjusted to their husbands' wishes. She could not understand this complex problem nor did she have the ability to analyse it. But she certainly had the sensitivity and compassion to wipe the tears of a hurt soul.

'Are you worried about your younger daughter Savita too?' she asked softly.

'Of course, I am. The elder sister is always the role model in the family. Some nights I am unable to sleep thinking Savita could do the same. At times, I feel enough is enough.

We should go back to Bangalore and settle there permanently. But Savita refuses to come. She says, if we want, we can go back, but she belongs to this country as she was born here.'

Gouramma felt a strange fear gnawing away at her mind. What if, after twenty years, Manasi behaved in the same way, causing great anguish to her son!

❦

Some time ago, Chandru had gone to California on work and was having coffee at a downtown restaurant in San Francisco. To his surprise, he saw Shama there, serving at another table. Though he was shocked, he did not show it. Shama behaved most normally.

'Hi Chandru uncle. What a surprise to see you here!' she greeted him.

Chandru invited her for dinner and she readily agreed to come with her boyfriend. Chandru was thinking of the different stages of Shama's life that he had been a witness to over the last ten years. He had seen her as a teenager, later as a young bride at her reception, radiant in a silk sari, and now she was a bold and confident young woman.

Chandru tactfully asked her in Kannada, 'What are your future plans, Shama?' but Shama replied in English. 'Uncle, please don't speak in Kannada, since Michael does not know the language. It is not polite. Though all of you are American citizens, your roots are in India, specifically in your home towns. You come to this country only to earn money but can never become a part of it. You want the best of both worlds, which is not possible. I know, in your mind you must be thinking that I don't have a proper job. But Michael's father will never think that. You people cheat yourself.'

Chandru did not ask any questions after that. The evening passed with Michael and Chandru having a pleasant and interesting conversation.

∽

And now Radhakrishna was confiding in Chandru.

'Chandru, I never came to America in search of wealth. I was in Delhi working as a scientist. I worked very hard and wrote some good research papers, which were later selected for an international conference. I could not afford to go on my own, and my boss always brought up one hurdle or the other to prevent my going officially because I did not belong to his community and did not speak his language. It was extremely frustrating, but I continued. When I was due for a promotion, they transferred me to a remote place in the northeast, where I could not continue with my research. I was thoroughly dejected and frustrated, so I decided to migrate to this country.'

'Are you happy here?' Chandru asked.

'As far as work is concerned, I am extremely happy. I don't have any complaints. When the winter sets in and it snows, I feel extremely uncomfortable. I still miss the mild winters of my home town, but otherwise, America has been more than fair to me. But on the personal side, I am unhappy because Savitri is unhappy. She insists that we should return to India. But I am scared to face the same life again. Moreover, only America can fund my expensive research.'

'America always attracts the best professionals,' Chandru said proudly.

'Come to think of it, Chandru, this is a funny country. Like a colourful web spun by a spider, an insect walks in and gets trapped. At first we are drawn by the best technology and the handsome remuneration. But once we stay here for some time, it is difficult to go back. We get used to the easy living conditions and the professional work atmosphere. The conditions in our country are far below what we expect. Sometimes I feel there are many good reasons to leave India, and it is much more difficult to go back and settle there after so many years.'

'You may be right. Statistics show that the majority of students who come to this country on a student visa stay back. Most of them are brilliant. Of late, though, some percentage of people do plan to go back because of the IT and biotech boom in India.'

'Our country is also so complex, you know. There is so much greed amongst our kith and kin. I built a bungalow in Bangalore. From buying the plot to the house-warming ceremony, everyone squeezed money out of us. Their attitude makes me sick.'

'Yes. Everyone there thinks that it is very easy to earn in dollars,' Chandru said. 'What they don't understand is that we also have to struggle, far away from home, family and culture. We worry about our children who are confused between the two value systems. Actually, the price you pay is very high. The Dollar is extremely expensive if you take into account all these points. All Indians back home only equate the dollar to forty-three or forty-five rupees.'

Chandru remembered an incident from his last visit to India. He was wearing a very expensive watch which Jamuna had given him for his birthday. His brother-in-law Suresh had liked it very much and repeatedly said, 'This is a very good watch. Next time, bring one for me and I will pay you the money.' Initially he had ignored the request, but when Suresh brought it up again, Gouramma had called Chandru inside and admonished him, 'Chandru, you earn in dollars. After all he is the son-in-law of the family. Give it to him.'

Chandru was unable to refuse his mother's demand. He knew that she would create a scene if he did not do what she asked. He removed the watch and gave it to Suresh, without uttering a word.

Coyly Suresh protested, 'Why are you gifting it to me? You can bring me one on your next visit. Anyway, Surabhi will give your mother the money.' But he promptly took the watch and slid it on to his wrist.

Chandru was well aware that Suresh would never pay the money but Gouramma would go about saying that he had.

After Chandru returned to America Jamuna noticed his bare wrist and he had had to explain what had happened. She flared up. 'Everyone in your family is greedy. They won't hesitate to strip a person naked and just grab all they can get from the US. Last time, your mother took away my bag and Surabhi helped herself to my cosmetic kit. They always have one mantra—"Anyway you can get it cheaper there." They don't realize that dollars do not grow on trees.'

In a fit of anger, she had not talked to him for a few days.

Another time, his Dharwad friend Kitty had sent an e-mail asking him to get a coral set for his wife and had promised that he would pay for it immediately. For old times' sake and much against Jamuna's wishes, Chandru had taken the set along. When he gave it, though, Kitty was very unhappy. 'This coral is not so red. It is rather pink. We get this kind even in India. Anyway, since you have brought it I will take it. After all it must have cost you just a few dollars.' Thus, he took it without paying for it.

U gadi, Kannada New Year, arrived quietly in America. Gouramma had taken the precaution of carrying a Hindu calendar along with her so as to keep track of all the important fasts and pujas. She was really happy to be there with her son for the festival, so she told Jamuna, 'New Year is on Thursday. Both of you take leave and let us celebrate it. Call your friends for lunch. We can go to the temple in the evening.'

Jamuna was completely untouched by her excitement. She replied, 'It's a working day, Amma. We get only a few days' leave in a year. We have to save it for emergencies. We cannot take leave for a festival. If you are keen, we will celebrate it on Sunday.'

'One can't celebrate festivals according to one's convenience . . . If it falls on a Thursday, we should observe it on that day. Vinuta always takes leave whenever we have a puja at home.'

Sarcastically Jamuna shot back, 'She is a government schoolteacher, which I am not. In any case, in India, people hardly work.'

Gouramma was at a loss for words. She just stared at Jamuna in silence as Jamuna walked off to her room.

༚

Gouramma had been observing the change in Jamuna's personality. She was such a different person in India, carefree, talkative, a spendthrift. But in the US, she was quieter, calculating and very conscious of her diet. She would drive twenty miles if she could get something for five dollars less.

Gouramma was disturbed on another account. She had noticed that, unlike Girish, Chandru had to share in the housework, and washing the dishes and ironing the clothes were his responsibilities. Gouramma had been brought up with the view that the male members of the household did not work in the kitchen.

'Chandru, please don't work in the kitchen. Don't you remember? Your father and Girish never come into the kitchen.'

Immediately Jamuna intervened. 'Don't pamper him, Amma. In India, you have servants. Even I had never stepped into a kitchen before I came here. Everybody has to share in the housework here.'

Gouramma was offended. 'Jamuna, I feel bad. As long as I am here, I will do Chandru's share of the work. When I leave, he can go back to sharing the workload.'

'What's the shame in doing work in your own house, Amma?' Jamuna retorted. 'Now because of Manasi, we have more work. Please do not give such advice.'

Gouramma's face fell. She felt hurt and humiliated. Chandru comforted his mother. 'Amma, you should not worry about such small things. Actually I enjoy helping out.'

'Can't you hire someone to iron your clothes?' Gouramma persisted. She felt awkward, when she saw her son ironing Jamuna's clothes.

'If I were rich like Jaya, then I could hire someone who can do the housework for ten dollars an hour. We are ordinary people,' said Jamuna.

Gouramma knew that there was no point in arguing. As it is, she was feeling miserable because this was the first

Ugadi festival where there were no mango or neem leaves strung on the front door, no puja of the *panchanga*, the Hindu calendar, no aroma of sweets and mango rice. To change the topic, she asked, 'Who is Jaya?'

'Jaya is Kishore's wife. They are one of the richest Indian families in the US. She celebrates Ugadi with a gala dinner. She invites all Indians and we too have an invitation for this weekend,' said Chandru.

'Does she invite people for all Hindu festivals?' Gouramma asked.

'No. The festivities are shared among different people. Some celebrate Deepavali and some others Sankranti, on the respective festival weekend. But all Indians meet.'

Everyone was looking forward to Jaya's party. Jamuna wore a very expensive silk sari, lots of jewellery, almost like a bride. Though Gouramma always liked the traditional Indian way of dressing, she felt that Jamuna was overdressed for the occasion, but she did not comment because Chandru was quiet. Gouramma had prepared some sweets which she carried in a big silver bowl.

Jaya's house was like a mansion, with a swimming pool, eight bedrooms and a huge lawn. Today the front hall was brightly decorated. There were many Indian children playing around, dressed in rich Indian costumes, speaking in an American accent. Most women were decked up like Jamuna. Gouramma felt that since these women never got an opportunity to wear Indian clothes they probably wanted to show off to each other. Most of the time, at work and at home, they wore practical Western outfits.

Feeling completely out of place in this crowd, Gouramma sat in a corner. A young woman with short hair, wearing a red Banarasi sari and sporting a bright red bindi on her forehead came up to her and spoke in

Kannada. 'Amma, you may not remember me. I am Chitra. I used to come to your house.' Was this well-built, confident girl the same thin, scared Chitra? Gouramma thought.

Chitra continued, 'I am Shankaranna's daughter. He was a peon in the school where Shamanna Sir taught. You had come along with him for my wedding and blessed me.'

Gouramma vaguely remembered something about Chitra's life and now she was a little confused. But Chitra continued talking, 'Why hasn't Sir come? Anyway, I am in a hurry now, but I will come and take you to my house tomorrow evening. Will you come? I will take the address from Jamuna.'

'Yes,' Gouramma agreed immediately. She desperately wanted a change.

It was a gala dinner; over a hundred people had been invited. Gouramma went up to Jaya and told her, 'You should have called me to help you. It must have been heavy work for you.'

'No, Aunty, I did not do any work. I called in caterers from New York.'

On the way home, Jamuna talked most enviously about Jaya. 'Oh yes, she has so much money, she wanted to flaunt it, that's why she called in caterers.' For some reason, Gouramma did not quite like that comment, but she couldn't put a finger on it. She felt they should appreciate Jaya for what she had done to get the Indian community together.

Just then she remembered her conversation with Chitra. Turning to Chandru she said, 'Chitra wants to take me to her house tomorrow evening. I would like to go.'

'Yes. Chitra Joseph took our address and the directions to our place,' added Jamuna.

Gouramma was puzzled. 'Chandru, Chitra was married to Manappa. How come she is a Joseph now?'

'Amma, I do not know anything about that lady except that she is from Bangalore. Anyway, don't ask any personal questions. People here do not like it,' said Chandru, familiar with his mother's inquisitive nature.

The next evening, Chitra came to pick up Gouramma, dressed in a casual Western outfit. She told Jamuna, 'I will take Amma with me now and drop her back after dinner.' Gouramma walked out to the car with her.

As they drove away, Chitra said, 'Amma, I feel as if my own mother is going to visit my house. We will stop at the Indian grocery store and pick up lots of Indian snacks. I'll buy you whatever you want.'

'No, Chitra. Food is not important to me. Milk and some fruit are fine. If you want to get a DVD you can stop there.'

'No, Amma. I don't need to watch DVDs. My life itself is a movie now. Don't you know that?'

'No,' said Gouramma, feigning nonchalance, but she was all ears.

'I was a very good student but you know what our circumstances were . . . Although I was very keen, I could not attend college. I got married when I was eighteen, to my second cousin Manappa who was ten years older than me. But my parents were happy that he had married me without any dowry.

'Manappa was a bad person. He drank all the time and harassed me. A year after my marriage, a drunken Manappa was knocked down by a lorry and I was back at my father's house.'

'I remember that you were attending typing class and I used to send your fees through my husband,' Gouramma recalled.

'Yes, Amma. Sir would always advise me, "Stand on your own feet, Chitra. One day it will help." You both gave my life a turn for the better. When I finished my course, I took up a job as a typist for a mere salary of three hundred rupees. By that time, my father had retired and we hardly met. I'm seeing you after such a long time.'

Gouramma remembered how Chitra had suffered in those days.

'I met Govind in my office; he was also a typist. We liked each other but when I told him I was a widow, his attitude changed. He became stiff and calculating. He said, "I will compromise and marry you, but you should give all your salary to me." Being the eldest in the family, I had to support my siblings, so I offered to give him half my salary but Govind did not agree. I felt so depressed and at times I felt like committing suicide. Around that time, I got a letter from Sowmya.'

'Who is Sowmya?'

'She was my boss's daughter. She and her husband Keshav were doctors in Los Angeles. After ten years of marriage, they had had twins. She wanted a domestic help, someone who was intelligent and efficient and could speak English. That brought me here.'

'How were they?'

'They were very nice. They paid for my ticket and sent my salary to my father. The first time I was so scared of air travel, and for a long time I was very homesick and craved to go back, even though it would mean a return to poverty.

'But Sowmya and her husband made me feel at home. And I loved the children and took care of them as if they were my own. I cannot express how indebted I am to Sowmya and Keshav.' Tears of gratitude flowed down

Chitra's cheeks. She suddenly realized that while narrating her life story she had overshot her house. She stopped and turned around.

'I attended evening courses and learnt driving. There I met Joseph. He is an American, an engineer by profession, and a year younger than me. His mother was a doctor. Both of us shared many common interests. So we decided to get married.'

'Did you tell him that you were a widow?' Gouramma asked.

'On the very first day. But he's not like Govind. He encourages me to work and send money to my parents. He is a large-hearted man.'

'What about your American mother-in-law? Have you got used to her?'

'We don't live with her. Though I was prepared to stay with her, such a system does not exist in America. But she loves me very much. We visit her on weekends. She has also made a trip to India to get to know my country and my people.'

When they reached home Joseph was waiting in the hall. Chitra introduced Gouramma.

'Hi, Gouramma,' he said in an American accent greeting her with a warm handshake. Gouramma felt a little awkward.

The house was peaceful, simple and full of contentment.

Joseph went inside and brought out milk and bananas for Gouramma, and laid out dinner plates for his wife and himself. In a most cordial atmosphere they had their dinner.

'Has your father ever visited you?' Gouramma asked Chitra.

'Not yet, but my parents are coming next year. Initially they were very upset that I was marrying Joseph. But now, they have accepted it. I send them five hundred dollars every month. My younger brother and sisters are all married and settled very well. So they have no worries now.'

Gouramma realized Chitra's migration to the US had benefited the entire family. If she had married Govind, he would have tortured her with nasty comments. Manappa had of course been useless. This white man, knowing that she was a widow, was a real human being.

When it was time to leave, Gouramma said, 'Chitra, bring some kumkum. I want to apply it on your forehead and bless you.'

With tears in her eyes Chitra brought a kumkum jar and Gouramma applied a nice red dot on her forehead. When Chitra bent down to touch her feet, Joseph joined her. 'May you live a hundred years with children and grandchildren in America,' Gouramma blessed the couple from the bottom of her heart.

Chitra gave Gouramma an ornament box and told her, 'Amma, I am not rich enough to fill this box with jewellery. I only pray that god will fill it up for you. I will never forget Sir's help in my time of need.'

For the first time, Gouramma felt proud of her husband. He may not have earned a lot of money, but his compassion and timely help had made such a big difference to the life of a person in trouble.

Six months had passed since Gouramma's arrival in America, and winter had given way to spring.

Chandru wanted to take his mother to New York, to show her another American city. Chandru and Jamuna had several friends in New York; there was also a Kannada Sangha and several temples. He thought his mother could do with a change.

When told, Gouramma was very enthusiastic. She began preparing sweets and savouries to carry for their various hosts in New York. Jamuna was also keen on the trip, as she wanted to do a lot of shopping. This would be her first vacation after the baby.

From the day Gouramma had arrived, Jamuna had not stepped inside the kitchen. In fact Chandru had once said worriedly, 'I think Amma is being overworked here.' But Gouramma had politely refuted this. 'No, I don't have anything else to do, this keeps me busy. It's fine.' She was happy to hear Chandru express his concern for her, but secretly, she wanted Jamuna to say such things. Jamuna too expressed her concern, but although she would say, 'Amma, tomorrow onwards you take rest. I will look after the kitchen. I will prepare Pongal,' those were only charming words; they were not followed by action.

On the drive to New York, Gouramma noticed how different the scenery was from the time that she had first arrived in America. All of nature had spread out its bounty;

flowers of a myriad colours were blooming. She thought how lucky she was that her son owned such a beautiful car. But when she heard Jamuna telling Chandru, 'I am tired of this old car, next year, we should buy a new car,' she realized that everyone had better cars and there was nothing special about Chandru's car.

While driving Chandru said, 'Amma, we are going to Shrikant's house. He is out of town. We can stay as long as we want. Keeping his house as a base, we can visit Rajiv, Mohan and others.'

'Who is Shrikant?'

'Shrikant was my senior colleague. His wife Roopa was a paediatric doctor from Chennai. But now they are divorced. He has gone to India to see his daughter who is with Roopa's parents.'

'Why did he divorce?' asked Gouramma.

'I am not sure what the problem was exactly, but people say it was because Roopa was earning more than him and she used to boss over him. He didn't like that and they used to fight. Finally they separated. Shrikant gave up his job and now has his own business. He has an office in India, so he shuttles between the two countries.'

'Now he must be making more money than his wife, I suppose?' said Jamuna.

'Maybe he is. I don't know.'

Chandru remembered something. 'Amma, we are going to meet Tara in Rajiv's house. Do not ask her anything personal like marriage or children.' Gouramma felt insulted at this admonition in front of her daughter-in-law and though she was curious to know about Tara, she felt she couldn't ask.

Jamuna said, 'I really feel that it was a marriage in a hurry and Tara was the victim.'

'Why?' Chandru countered. 'We also got married in a short time. It is just Tara's bad luck.'

Seeing the look of curiosity on his mother's face, Chandru continued, 'Tara was married to Ramesh who was a family friend's son. Tara's parents had sold their property in order to give her a lavish wedding. After the wedding, Tara came to the US and she learnt that Ramesh was already married to a white girl and had a son. She decided to get a divorce but did not want to go back to India. After the divorce, though, she did not know what to do. She was trained to be a good homemaker, not a professional. So she now works part-time in a library. She's related to Rajiv, which is why she'll be there this weekend at Rajiv's place.'

'What did Tara's father-in-law say?' asked Gouramma.

'He asked for forgiveness and scolded his son but what was the point? He too was innocent and knew nothing of his son's deceitfulness. Ramesh puts the blame on his father, saying that he married because of family pressure. It is better to verify the details before the marriage than suffering later.'

'Yes, I agree. My father had enquired discreetly about you too, before putting forth the proposal,' Jamuna proudly spoke of her father.

Gouramma thought of the time she had been so angry with Vinuta for having made enquiries about Shekhar, and how she and Surabhi had abused her. Surabhi's life could have been like Tara's, and thank god she had been saved this kind of humiliation.

'Chandru, why shouldn't Tara marry Shrikant? Both are divorcees anyway.' Gouramma made a quick proposal.

Keeping his eyes on the traffic, Chandru mused, 'Amma, after staying here for so many years, we absorb this culture without realizing it. Though Shrikant is my close friend, I do not interfere in his life. In this country, everyone loves the complete freedom of their private life. Even parents do not ask personal questions of their children. There is an invisible line in any relationship. And no one wants to cross it. They don't mind sacrificing anything for their privacy. Sometimes it ends up in divorce.'

'Tara knows Shrikant and if they find each other compatible, they will decide about marriage. They are grown up and we should not even suggest it,' said Jamuna.

It still did not make sense to Gouramma.

They reached Shrikant's house in the early afternoon. To their surprise, a young woman was waiting for them. Lunch was served on the table—fresh, hot food in beautiful casseroles and neatly arranged cutlery.

She introduced herself. 'Please come in. I am Malati. My husband works for Shrikant. He has gone out. We received an e-mail about your arrival. So I thought I would prepare some food for you while you are here. I have to cook for the two of us anyway, so I can easily cook for three more.'

Malati had kept the house very neat and tidy. After lunch, everyone retired to their rooms. Gouramma never slept in the afternoons. She went in search of Malati, to chat with her, and found her in the kitchen preparing snacks for teatime. There was another woman helping her in the kitchen. Gouramma immediately said, 'Don't exert yourself, Malati. I have brought lots of eatables from home.'

'Don't worry, Aunty. Martha is my helper in my shop. When the shop is closed, she helps me in the kitchen. Though she is a Colombian immigrant, I have trained her in all south Indian cooking,' Malati said proudly, smiling at Martha in appreciation.

'Then you are a businesswoman!'

'Yes, but not a very big one. I run the shop from my house. I buy fancy stuff from India, like beaded handbags, embroidered chappals, silk scarves, Banarasi cushion covers, dhurries, brass lamps, small idols of different gods, etc., and sell them here.'

'Who are your customers?

'Mostly Indians. Not everyone can afford to go to India every year. So my shop is convenient for them. Similarly, I have one more shop in India. There I sell corals, jade, Spanish saffron, cinnamon, etc.'

'So you keep shuttling between India and the US?'

'Yes. Whenever Shrikant is in India, my husband and I are here and when he is here, we are generally in India. In my absence, Martha looks after the shop. In India, my brother looks after that shop. Normally we commute three times a year.'

'What does your husband do?'

'My husband is an ordinary graduate like me. He was a medical rep before coming here. We are honest and work very hard. In three years, we have made good money. Now we are building a shopping complex in Jayanagar. This country rewards those who work hard. We are both extremely happy and admire and appreciate this country. It has changed our life. No wonder people call this a land of nectar and honey. That's why when people criticize the US, we get mad.'

'We too are from Jayanagar. Who are your in-laws?'

'My father-in-law is a retired postmaster. My husband Gopinath is well known in his area, because of his involvement in all extra-curricular activities.'

Just then, the telephone rang and Malati went to attend to it. Gouramma was shaken. This was the very same boy whom Gouramma had forced Surabhi to stop associating with. She had always felt that her daughter should have plenty of money. Today, Malati was enjoying all that. She remembered how Girish had been positive about Gopinath but she had been blind. She sighed deeply.

The next day Chandru took them to see the Statue of Liberty, the Rockefeller Center, some temples and then they went to Padma's house.

Gouramma was amazed at the temples in America. There were temples of all the gods in one complex, unlike India. Chandru explained, 'Earlier there was only the Venkateshwara temple in Pittsburgh. Now, due to the software boom, lots of professionals come here from different parts of India. It is difficult to build a separate temple for each deity. That's why you find Hanuman, Ganesha, Kumaraswamy, Rama and Sita, Shiva-Parvati, Lakshmi, all in one temple.'

'But what about the priests?'

'They are normally imported from India. They get a special visa for five years. In their free time, they also help perform functions like naming ceremonies, marriages, etc., in some houses.'

As it was a holiday, there were streams of devotees, but still the temple premises were absolutely clean and orderly. The floors were shining. There was a reserved car park for the handicapped, and waste paper baskets were neatly lined up. Gouramma felt Indian gods looked brighter under the sparkle of American cleanliness.

The prasad was distributed in the temple office. Though there were devotees of different colours, features and languages, all Indians were connected by the same string of devotion. In one corner of the temple, there was a wedding ceremony being performed. A Hindu boy was getting married to an American girl. In another corner, the thread ceremony of a Tamil boy was being conducted. The American-born and brought up child was finding it hard to recite and repeat the Sanskrit slokas. For Gouramma, this was all a very new experience.

When they reached Padma's home, Gouramma felt more at home. Padma was a warm and hospitable person and had wholeheartedly agreed to host them though she was in an advanced stage of pregnancy. She already had a three-year-old son, Vivek.

The following day Padma told Jamuna and Chandru, 'Please leave Amma for three or four days with me. We are going to have a get-together of Kannadigas. Rajiv will be visiting Nashville this weekend and he can drop her back.' Rajiv joined his wife in the persuasive invitation. 'Chandru, I am going to Paris on some work for the next three days and Padma will be alone. They will be good company for each other. I take personal responsibility to see that your mother reaches home safely.'

Jamuna did not like this idea. She said, 'Amma may get bored here. She does not know anybody, and Manasi will miss her.'

I can't be with you forever. Let me have my freedom, Gouramma felt like shouting at the top of her voice, but restrained herself.

In spite of Jamuna's protest, Chandru agreed to leave Gouramma with Rajiv and Padma.

Jamuna left in a bad mood.

Vatsala, one of Padma's friends, came to visit and brought along a box of sweets. She said, 'Padma, I thought you were alone so I came to enquire about you.'

Introducing Gouramma, Padma said, 'Thanks, but Aunty is with me. If I need anything, I will surely let you know.'

Vatsala left immediately.

'Vatsala could have stayed back for dinner. What was the hurry? Padma, when I am here you can call any guests over for lunch or dinner. I will help you.'

'Normally Vatsala does not visit many people. She is a top executive and extremely busy.'

'She must be highly educated. Is she from Bangalore?'

'Actually she only studied till the tenth standard when in India. Her father was a rich merchant in Bidar. They were very orthodox. So she was married off when she was sixteen years old. Her husband was working in the US. When she came here, she had a baby very soon, but she also worked very hard. She went on to complete her graduation and later finished an MBA. Today, she is one of the top women achievers. She is one of the very few women who have succeeded so well in a faraway land, and that too, after marriage.'

'What is so great about that? Even in India, many women study after marriage.'

'But here, there is no family support system. Vatsala single-handedly did all the work. Since here you can study whatever you want, at any age, she took advantage of the system. Also, in the US there are very few unannounced visitors dropping in to chat, so she could pursue her studies diligently. She not only worked at home and took care of her son, she did very well in her course. Her son, Ashok, is a very well-behaved boy. Largely, there is a fair system of appreciation. Because it is a country of immigrants, you see people from all over the world. There is practically no discrimination at work.'

'Is Ashok staying with his parents?'

'No. He stays separately, but in the neighbourhood.'

'Why? Has he fought with his parents?'

'No, no. But here, when the children grow up, parents feel they should be independent and learn the ways of life by themselves. Children also prefer it. Children visit their parents during the weekends.'

'What happens when parents grow old?'

'As long as they are healthy and independent, they stay independently. If they are unable to, then they go to some old age home. There they have the advantage of mixing with people of their own age. People here don't think of living in an old age home as punishment.'

Gouramma clicked her tongue. She could not understand this very different world.

That night, Padma felt uneasy, although there were still a couple of weeks till her due date. First, she got up and called the hospital. Gouramma heard a sound and got up too. Padma was preparing her bag to go to the hospital. Gouramma asked, 'Should I pack it for you?'

'No, thanks Aunty. It's easier for me to do it since I know where everything is kept.'

'Should I call Vatsala to drop you to the hospital?'

'No. I have already called the ambulance.'

'Can I massage some oil on your stomach?'

'No, that is not required.'

'Can I get you some coffee or tea?'

'No. It is better to be on an empty stomach.'

Gouramma felt helpless. None of her advice or help seemed to be of any use.

'Shall I light the oil lamp in front of the god?'

'No, Aunty. It is a wooden case. You can switch on the electric lamp.'

'Please inform Rajiv.'

'I have already done that.'

The ambulance arrived and Padma walked to it with a small bag. Even in a moment like this she remembered to say, 'Aunty, don't worry about me. I had registered my name in the hospital long back. They will take care of everything. You stay with Vivek. Don't send him to school tomorrow. Write down each call. This is unexpected labour. I am very happy that it came while you are here. It is a great comfort to me. I am sorry if you are finding it inconvenient.' Waving, Padma went away to hospital.

Such a wealthy country, and a pregnant woman had to go to the hospital all alone! No one had the time to accompany her. Everyone was just too busy with their own lives. Their dedication to their jobs was amazing. But, the flip side was that loneliness was growing, human bonds were weakening. Gouramma was unable to sleep. She prayed for a safe delivery.

Early in the morning, Padma called and told Gouramma that she had delivered a baby boy. Rajiv and Chandru had already spoken to her in the meantime.

Rajiv cut his trip short and returned the very next day. As Padma had delivered on a working day, there were hardly any visitors at the hospital.

Gouramma stayed on for another week and looked after Padma when she came home from the hospital. Padma was deeply touched by the affection with which Gouramma took care of her.

Jamuna kept calling her mother-in-law, asking her to return. When Rajiv was due to take her back, Padma handed over an envelope to Gouramma. 'I wanted to buy a sari for you. I will never forget the way you looked after me, just like my mother. Please buy a sari in India and think of me as your daughter.'

Gouramma was moved to tears.

B y the time she returned from New York, Gouramma's
perception of America had changed a lot. She was
missing her country. That month, she wrote out a list and
gave it to Chandru. She had lost all interest in going to the
grocery store or to any other store.

A few days after her return from New York, Chandru
told his mother, 'Amma, every Thursday I have a meeting
at an office which is close to Bombay Grocery Store, the
Indian store. Why don't you come with me and buy
whatever you want?'

'Can I leave Manasi at home while she is sleeping and
lock the house? Will we be back soon?'

'That is not allowed in this country. Even if she is
sleeping, bring her to the shop with you.'

Reluctantly Gouramma went to the Indian store.

Bombay Grocery Store was like any other Indian grocery
store, packed with DVDs, vegetables, ready-to-eat food
packets, different types of masalas, pickles, etc. The freezer
was stuffed with palak paneer, samosas and batata vada.
Gouramma realized one didn't need to bring anything from
India; everything was available in the US. She wondered
why Jamuna always insisted that Gouramma send masala
powders from India.

When Chandru dropped her at the store, Gouramma
panicked. How would she translate Kannada words into
English? While she was struggling, the lady across the
counter spoke. 'I can understand Kannada. Don't worry.'

The woman was in her mid-thirties, and extremely active. She talked on a phone while she juggled some items. Gouramma realized that she was making tea.

'Would you like some tea, Aunty?' she asked pleasantly.

Gouramma declined politely, then added, 'What is your name?'

'Asha Patil.'

'How do you manage all the work?' Gouramma asked, impressed by her efficiency.

'I work in the store from 11.00 a.m. to 3.00 p.m. My husband is here from 3.00 to 7.00. We alternate our duties.'

'What do you do at home?'

'I have two Gujarati women helpers. I get chapattis made. I also prepare samosas and other eatables.'

'You must be busy all day.'

'Yes. But then, money doesn't come easily, does it?'

Though Gouramma wanted to know more about her, by this time she had learned that asking too many questions was considered bad manners.

Thus it became her routine every Thursday—Gouramma would bring Manasi and spend an hour with Asha Patil at Bombay Grocery Store. Gouramma liked Asha's straightforward manner and affectionate behaviour.

During one such visit, Gouramma casually asked, 'How long have you been here?'

'Ten years.'

'Don't you feel homesick?' asked Gouramma, a manifestation of her own feelings.

There was no answer forthcoming at once.

Asha went inside, brought two cups of coffee for them, and sat down. There were no customers in the shop.

'I hail from a village near Akkalkot, near the border between Maharashtra and Karnataka. We speak Kannada at home and Marathi outside. We are a middle-class family and we own some land. I have two younger brothers. I was a strong young girl, so soon after I finished my matriculation exams, somebody in our village brought an alliance for me. They told us that the boy, Satish Patil, was in Bombay and was making good money in his business. My parents were gullible, and without any verification, they got me married off. After I came to Mumbai, I realized that my husband's family lived in one room in a chawl. I had an extraordinarily bad mother-in-law and three even worse sisters-in-law. My husband owned a bhel-puri cart. The family got a free servant in marriage. I would work like a donkey all day long. My husband did not have a backbone and I suffered a lot.'

Her face saddened, as she recalled the past. Yet when one or two customers walked in, she attended to them very pleasantly.

'Our daughter Vinaya was born. I always used to dream that I would live in a house with an affectionate mother-in-law and sisters-in-law and a loving husband. I would own a small house with a small garden in which my child would play . . . there would be peace and happiness around me.

'But there was a vast difference between reality and imagination. The house was always noisy—fighting and shouting. I went into a depression. My in-laws thought I was acting, that I was being lazy. But one day my father came to visit me, realized my state, and took me back to my village. He had me treated at a good hospital in Miraj. Slowly I started recovering. It took almost two years. After that I refused to go back to my in-laws' house. My father had a Gujarati friend whose relative wanted to open a hotel along with a grocery shop in New York. He told my father that they were looking for a hard-working couple, and my father felt it was a good opportunity for us.'

'Did your husband agree to come with you?'

'Of course. Once I said America, he agreed immediately. We became illegal immigrants and worked in New York for some time. Afterwards, we regularized our immigrant status. We worked from morning to evening in the kitchen. Still, life was better than in Mumbai. I gradually understood how the business ran. So one day I took the lead and requested our employer Arunbhai to allow us to start out on our own. He was upset at first, but later, he agreed. Thus, we started Bombay Store here. However, I still buy all the groceries wholesale from Arunbhai.'

'How do you feel now?'

'I feel great. This county has changed my life forever. There are no signs of depression at all. What I used to dream about has come true. My husband was listening to his mother before but now he is devoted to me. We helped financially for all my sisters-in-law's weddings but I never visit them. My father had taken a loan for my treatment. I have returned that loan. I have also helped my brothers to start businesses. It is only because of this country that all this has been possible. There are many women like me in India, tortured by their mothers-in-law. But they do not have any option. Sometimes, they commit suicide, sometimes they run away and some get into depression. For me, god helped in the form of America. I am extremely happy here and I don't feel like going back.'

'Are you not worried about your daughter, when she comes to marriageable age?" Gouramma asked.

'No. What is going to happen with other girls here will happen to my daughter too. I know many Indian girls who have far more loose morals than American girls. Here, everything is in the open, but in India, since society does not accept such things, they do them anyway without the knowledge of their parents.'

Gouramma's mind was reeling. She felt she was seeing the world from a new perspective.

twenty-five

O ne day Chandru said, 'Amma, the button on my shirt has come off. Could you please stitch it on today?' Gouramma usually did all such minor work during the afternoons. She hunted around for a sewing kit, and was surprised when she could not find one. She thought it may be in Jamuna's wardrobe. Gouramma had never opened Jamuna's wardrobe. She respected Jamuna's privacy. When she opened the wardrobe in her hunt for the sewing kit, she saw a lot of saris in one corner and a pile of photo albums in the other. She located the kit underneath the photo albums, and just as she pulled out the small kit, the albums tumbled and fell.

As she busily gathered them up, some pictures which had fallen out of the albums caught her eye. There was a picture of Jamuna and Chandru at Niagara Falls. What caught Gouramma's eyes was not the spectacular beauty of the Falls but what Jamuna was wearing. Gouramma immediately recognized it as the same chiffon sari which Jamuna had gifted Surabhi for her birthday during one of her visits. Curious, Gouramma looked through all the photographs very carefully. She recognized several of the saris Jamuna was wearing in the pictures.

Gouramma was shocked. When Jamuna had said, 'I specially brought these saris for you since they will suit your colour,' Gouramma had praised her to the skies for her generosity. Gouramma preferred American saris as they did not fade even after frequent washing: they remained fresh. She now realized Jamuna had cleverly got rid of many of her old saris and had received so much appreciation and gratitude for that.

How could Jamuna have behaved like this? There was nothing inherently wrong in passing on a used sari but, Gouramma felt, one should not lie about it. Jamuna had done it all so cleverly that even if Gouramma accused her of giving away old saris, she could always say, 'Oh, I bought you an identical sari' or 'Where is the proof?' and create a scene. But worse was to follow. Gouramma found a photograph taken at Jamuna's cousin's wedding. Jamuna and her mother had posed along with the bride, both in expensive silk saris. The same saris had been ironed and professionally folded and gifted to Surabhi at her wedding. Gouramma was furious. She thought to herself, I was crazy about all American things and expensive silks, but it does not mean that I will accept a used sari as a gift.

She was deeply hurt and decided that never again would she ask Jamuna for anything from America.

~

Normally, Jamuna and her friends got together every Saturday. The idea was to have fun for four or five hours, play games, discuss an interesting novel or poetry, exchange news and gossip and go home after a sumptuous lunch. It was usually a potluck party, with everyone bringing a dish.

Chandru was away at New York that Saturday, and Jamuna organized the get-together at her home. Jamuna told her mother-in-law, 'Let us make idli–sambar. I will help you.' By this time, Gouramma knew what that meant. She felt she was only a servant in her son's house and everything had to be decided by her Dollar Bahu.

After she finished the cooking, Gouramma put everything on the table and decided to take Manasi for a stroll. Manasi was nearly ten months old.

Gouramma was still very upset by what she had found out about Jamuna. She had always praised her Dollar Bahu to high heaven but now realized how undeserving Jamuna was of that praise. After a long walk, Gouramma returned home. Manasi was asleep in her stroller. When she reached the door, Gouramma heard her name and stopped for a minute. She was curious to know what Jamuna and her friends were saying about her. Foolishly she thought, maybe Jamuna is praising my services.

She listened in on the conversation. Girija said, 'Jamuna, you are the smartest of all. I can trade my PhD to possess your talent on how to handle a mother-in-law and win her heart.'

'It seems her mother-in-law always treats her like her own daughter! Is it not surprising?' said Veda.

'Nothing so surprising. My mother-in-law is greedy and stupid. My co-sister-in-law Vinuta is from a poor family and innocent about the ways of the world. My sis-in-law Surabhi does not have any brains. It is easy to manage such women.'

Gouramma began sweating. Her Dollar Bahu continued spewing out her real feelings. 'I give them what I don't like and they don't suspect anything. For example, I pass on all my old saris to Surabhi and I tell her, due to customs restrictions, I rewrapped them. They believe me. My mother-in-law cannot understand that she should get along with Vinuta who slogs day and night for these people but instead, she praises me. I always believe in divide and rule.'

'Jamuna, I don't know why we should take anything from here. Nowadays we get everything in India. Last time,

I played a trick. I went to Burma Bazaar where we get all imported stuff, much cheaper than in the US, without warranty. I purchased some things for a few thousand rupees and told everyone at home that I had brought them from America. Everybody was very happy,' said Girija.

'No wonder you go with an empty suitcase from here. You are also quite smart,' Jamuna complimented her.

'Jamuna, are you planning to go back to India sometime?'

'No way! Here our husbands listen to us; we can eat, drink, dress and roam around the way we want. It is better to send some dollars as gifts than to settle in India. My father had clearly told me that he agreed to the proposal only because Chandru was in America, otherwise he would not have bothered. My parents had already judged these people before they accepted the proposal. My mother advised me to be nice, speak to them well, but keep them at a distance. That advice has helped.'

Rohini said, 'If you really calculate and get someone from India at the time of delivery, it is so advantageous.'

Jamuna immediately replied, 'That is why I wanted my mother-in-law for one year. She was dying to come to the US anyway, and my husband wanted his mother to come. It was at the right time that I called for her. In this one year, she has looked after us, the house and baby sat Manasi.'

'And one doesn't need to worry about anyone stealing either. The cost of the ticket is nothing, once you add up all these benefits,' added Rekha.

Gouramma couldn't bear it any more. She collapsed on the steps with her head in her hands. Oh god! Why was I so stupid? she cursed herself. Her head began to throb. For the first time she felt that her husband was a clever man for not coming here. She felt like running away to India immediately. She also realized that she had married her son off to an evil-minded person, falling prey to her wealth and sweet talk.

Just then Manasi woke up and began to demand attention. Gouramma picked up the child and went into the living room. Jamuna got up with a sweet smile and told her, 'Everyone says you have a magic line in your hand and no five-star hotel can compete with your sambar.' Gouramma did not even smile. She quietly went to her room.

That entire night Gouramma cried, and her wet pillow was testimony to her uncontrollable grief. She missed Vinuta. Now she could finally appreciate that poor girl. She regretted her own attitude towards Vinuta. She felt awful when she remembered that she had never even given Vinu any gift, be it for her pregnancy or on any other occasion, and how badly she had treated her in the run-up to Surabhi's wedding.

How blind I was! Why did I behave so stupidly? she kept asking herself through that wretched night. And the answer became clear. It was the Dollar. The Dollar had blinded her, making her unable to see the reality.

The next morning she spoke to Chandru. 'Manasi is old enough to go to a day-care centre. It is almost a year since I have been away from home. Your father must be lonely. It is better that I go back.'

'Please do not go now. It seems there is acute water shortage in Bangalore and the power supply is very irregular. After a few months, I will take you to California and Disneyland. You will enjoy that,' Jamuna tried to coax her mother-in-law to stay on, not aware that she had seen through her ways.

'No. I want to go back. I am getting bored here. How long can anyone stay away from home? My place is in India and I feel comfortable there, in spite of all the difficulties.'

'Yes, Jamuna, let her go. She has helped us so much; we should not hold her back any more. I will ask around for someone who is going to Bangalore soon.'

That evening, when Chandru returned from office he said, 'Amma, do you know Shanta, daughter of Alamelu? It seems Alamelu was your friend.'

'Of course I know Alamelu. We were neighbours when we were children. Shanta is Girish's age. Don't you remember her? She used to play with you when we went to Ajji's house during the holidays. Where is Alamelu now?'

'I don't remember. But today I met Shanta and while talking, I spoke about you and she remembered you at once. She wants to talk to you.'

Just then, Shanta called. 'Chandru, I am leaving the gym now. I can pick up your mom. She can stay the night with me, and I'll drop her back tomorrow evening. Ask her whether she is okay with it?'

Gouramma agreed immediately, and started packing an overnight bag. 'Why does Shanta go to a gym?'

'To exercise, to keep her body in good shape. I am planning to join,' said Jamuna.

'There's no need to go to a gym to get into shape. Doing housework will keep you fit. Vinuta never backs out from doing any housework and she has never put on an extra kilo, even after delivery. She is slim, without going to any gym.'

Jamuna was surprised to hear something positive about Vinuta from Gouramma for the first time.

When Shanta arrived, the first question Gouramma asked was, 'What happened? You had such lovely long hair!'

'Aunty, with so much to do, it is difficult to maintain such long hair. So I have cut it short.'

'Vinuta has thick long hair. She manages to maintain it with regular oiling and washing, though she is also a working lady.'

This came as another shock to Jamuna.

Without a word to Jamuna, Gouramma got into the car. During the drive she sat silently having learnt not to ask personal questions.

Shanta's house was not a bungalow. It was a two-bedroom house in a residential complex. It was a simple, ordinary house with the bare minimum of everything. On a stand, there was a picture of Shanta and her daughter. Shanta warmed the food in the microwave and put it on the dining table for the two of them.

Gouramma asked, 'Where is your daughter?'

'She is in school in India.'

'How is your husband?'

'Oh, that is a long story. I was married to Mukund after my graduation. You know that we were five sisters and Appa was quite worried about our marriage. Mukund was working in a software company, in a small job. After marriage, I started working in the same company and I was smarter than Mukund. So I got promotions faster than he did. My daughter Lata was born then.

'My company sent me here on an assignment. I brought in Mukund and Lata. Mukund expected that I should be a dutiful wife and also developed a complex because he had to report to me. We had constant fights. As he earned less than me, he would draw money from my account without my knowledge and make merry. The day I came to know, we fought and separated. He was unable to stand the fact that his wife earned more than he did. He always compared me with some other women and taunted me that they were good women because they served their husbands well. He had too much of a male ego and it was difficult to stay with him. Now, Lata is in Ooty and I visit her once a year. I will bring her here for her college education. I am saving every penny for that. That is the reason I live so frugally.'

Gouramma felt saddened, but Shanta continued brightly, 'I am happy in this country. This society does not look down upon single women—unmarried, divorced or widowed. They don't gossip behind your back. Nobody asks personal questions. If I do well, I will earn more money. I am contented. These difficulties have made me face the realities and I no longer need a protective shelter.'

The next morning, Shanta dressed in a typical south Indian sari and escorted Gouramma around the temples nearby.

Later in the evening she dropped her back at Chandru's place.

'Amma, my friend Vinod Shah's parents would like to meet you.'

'I do not know their language and they are not native to our place. What will I do meeting them?' Gouramma frowned.

'I am going to Rekha's house for a party. We will drop you off at Vinod's place and Chandru will go to the library. All of us can then return together.' Jamuna had given her verdict.

Gouramma had no choice but to agree. She did not want to hurt her son during the last few days of her stay. When they reached Vinod's house, his wife Meera was feeding her pet cat with some fishbones in the garden. She smiled at them and said, 'Vinod has gone to his mother's house.'

Chandru turned the car around, and while driving, he said, 'Vinod's parents stay separately because Madhuriben and Meera cannot get along. There is no point in staying together if you are going to fight.'

'In that case, why do they have to stay here? They can pretty well go back to India!' exclaimed Gouramma.

'He is the only son and they do not have any other option,' said Chandru. Gouramma mentally thanked god that she had another son back in India.

Madhuriben and her husband were waiting for Gouramma. She had prepared a lot of Gujarati sweets for the guest. Vinod left with Chandru for the library.

Madhuriben began to speak in Hindi, which fortunately Gouramma could follow. She said, 'How lucky you are that you are going back to India. My mind always thinks of Gujarat, our festivals, our old house, the children around, our garba festivals. But we do not have much option and have to stay here.

'This country is meant for youngsters and not for people like us. We have spent our best years in India. We feel uprooted at this age. But then, if we stay in India and one of us falls ill, Vinod has to come all the way and it is such an expense. The only way is to stay with him and make it easier for him and for us.'

Vinod told Chandru that he was going to Bangalore and Gouramma decided to fly back with him.

Jamuna told Gouramma, 'We are sad to see you go, Amma. If you want to buy anything for Surabhi, please let me know.'

Gouramma said firmly, 'We get everything in India now. In fact, we can get a Mysore silk for the same price you pay for a chiffon sari.' She refused to take any gifts from Jamuna. She had the money Padma had given her, two hundred dollars, so she bought purses for Vinuta and Surabhi and some toys for Harsha. She would miss Manasi terribly—but then, life had to go on. As the day of her departure approached, Gouramma became more enthusiastic about her return. She was aware that she would never visit America again and she felt sorry for Chandru, who had to put up with such a wife, so far from home. But that again was each person's fate, she consoled herself.

When the flight landed in Bangalore, for the first time in a year Gouramma felt at home. She realized that the grass was always greener on the other side. America was no longer a fantasy land for her. There was pain, misery and happiness there, as in any other country. It was no longer the land of the mighty Dollar, which made magic. It was not paradise.

Shamanna had come to receive her at the airport. He had hired a taxi. She wondered why Girish had not come to receive her, which she had fully expected. Shamanna gently explained, 'I shall tell you everything once we get home. How was America?'

'It was fine. We shall talk about it at home.'

Gouramma was delighted to see the familiar scenes: cycles, rickshaws, street hawkers, the dust and heat.

Shamanna said, 'I thought America would never let you go. How come you are back in a year?'

'America is great but our country is no less. Tell me, how are Vinuta and Harsha? Did they miss me?'

Shamanna turned around and stared at Gouramma. He could not believe his ears.

Presently, they reached home.

Vinuta always worried that she had never been a good daughter-in-law in Gouramma's eyes, her best efforts notwithstanding. Now, she was more worried that after a year-long stay in America, Gouramma would treat her more like dirt. She knew that Girish would never back her; he always had a standard answer: 'Amma is like that. You cannot change her at this age. She respects Chandru more than she does me, but I don't mind. After all he is my brother.' Vinuta knew from past experience that any discussion on this matter with Girish was a waste of time. So she had to be prepared to listen to Gouramma singing Jamuna's praises every day. She sank into a depression as Gouramma's arrival drew nearer.

Vinuta also felt that there would now arise a new complication—constant comparisons between Manasi and Harsha. Harsha would grow up with a complex because Manasi was a Dollar granddaughter. She began to hate the word 'dollar'. She felt that if she were in America, she could also have come home once in three years and everybody would have praised her to high heaven. She prayed to god, Let a day come when forty-five dollars are equal to one rupee. If that did happen, what would this Dollar Bahu do!

Vinuta wanted to escape this atmosphere of constant comparison and unfair judgement. She kept brooding about America and its strange effects on people. Shankar had loved Shashi, and their marriage had been fixed. For a green card he had broken the alliance. Surabhi had ditched Gopi because he did not have prospects of going to America. What kind of power was this? she wondered.

Shamanna guessed what was going on in Vinuta's mind. One day he called her to his room and said, 'Vinu, I want to tell you a story.'

Vinuta was surprised, but then she thought that it was probably an incident from his younger days, many of which Shamanna had already narrated, and often.

'Vinuta and Kadru were the two wives of Sage Kashyap,' began Shamanna. 'There was tough competition between them. The condition was such that the one who lost would become the other's slave until her son brought back the holy nectar. Kadru cheated and won, and Vinuta became the slave. A hundred years later, however, Vinuta's son Garuda brought in the nectar and rescued his mother from slavery.'

'Why are you telling me this story, Appa?'

'All due to my wife's foolish behaviour, you will develop a complex and you will start hating our family the way a slave does. If the woman of the house is unhappy, a family can never live in peace. Vinuta, I do not want you to live with such a complex. In that story, the son comes after a good hundred years. I don't want you to stay in this house for that long, in bondage. Please go away and make your own home.'

Vinuta was surprised by this sudden decision.

'Is Girish aware of this?'

'Yes. I have told him the same thing and have explained the situation. Chandru, being away from us, has become independent, assertive and confident. I want Girish also to become like that. He is always under the protection of his parents. In that sense, America has taught Chandru a good lesson.'

'Appa, what type of country is America?' Vinuta asked in wonder. America had been haunting her of late.

'How do I know, Vinu? I have never been there. But based on common sense, I can only be grateful that many of our comforts were bought by the purchasing power of dollars. It has done a lot for us. We are now financially better off. Many lower-middle-class families have benefited from their children going to America. Many parents have been able to see some comforts in life because their children have settled there. They have been able to build houses, and marry off their dughters without too much trouble. Look at Gouri, her desires were mostly fulfilled because of Chandru. But she does not understand that money is not everything in life. There are other problems.'

'What are the problems, Appa?'

'Nothing comes for free, Vinu. And definitely not when it comes to financial help. This Dollar may have transformed the lifestyles of some families, taken them from poverty to wealth, but it has also broken up some families. It has created financial and social distinctions within families and destroyed peace of mind. Very few people have understood this. If Gouri had been more mature, she would not have been in awe of the Dollar and danced to its tune. Her greed burnt the peace and harmony in our family. Sometimes I get upset with her but when I think rationally, the poverty during her childhood, lack of education, the sudden surge of money, have obviously affected her. Gouri is not a bad human being, but she is misguided. I am sure she will realize that the enchanted forest is a mirage, but I am afraid it might be too late by then.'

'Appa, what do you think? Is America better than India or is India better than America?'

Shamanna smiled. 'There is no such thing, my child. For that matter, nothing is absolute in life. America has a set of advantages and disadvantages. Similarly, India has its own. You cannot have the best of both worlds. If you have a choice, choose a country and accept it with its pluses and minuses and live happily there. Staying in America and dreaming of an Indian way of life, or living in India and expecting an American way of life—both are roads to grief.'

Vinuta was silent for a long time, pondering over what Shamanna had said. Then coming back to the present, she said, 'Appa, where can we go?'

'I have told Girish to apply for a transfer to Dharwad. I have also sent him to the government education office with a request for your transfer. The person in charge was my student. I am sure that he will comply with my request. You have your own house there and you will love to live there as you did before. You need not send us any money. I plan to tell Chandru, too, to stop sending us dollars. With just the two of us, we can rent out the first floor. And I have my pension. We can lead a comfortable, peaceful life without being a burden on our children.'

Vinuta looked at her father-in-law. She felt sad that just when he was ageing, and when it was proper that his children should stay with him, they would be leaving him.

'Appa, will you not come and stay with us?'

'Of course we will. And you will visit us. But for the moment, do not wait until Gouri's return. Go and set up your house. My blessings are always with you.'

❦

Sudha Murty

The taxi stopped in front of their house and Shamanna opened the door with his keys.

'Today is Sunday. How come Vinuta is not at home?'

'She is not in Bangalore. She has shifted to Dharwad, on transfer.'

'What? How can she leave Girish and go?' Gouramma was upset.

'He has also been transferred to Dharwad.'

'How can they go without my permission?'

'They are adults. They do not require our permission. As a matter of fact, it was I who sent them. Your fulsome praise of Jamuna was pushing Vinu into a depression; the symptoms were there to be seen. I do not want my healthy daughter-in-law to suffer for no fault of hers. It is better that she be away from such an atmosphere.'

Somewhere in the corner of her mind, Gouramma was reminded of Asha Patil.

'Gouri, love and affection are more important than food and money. Vinuta is like our daughter and I do not want her to suffer. What I would have done for Surabhi, I did for Vinuta.'

Gouramma sat down helplessly. 'Gouri, we raised our children according to our ideas and values,' Shamanna continued quietly. 'Now, allow Vinuta to do the same thing in her house. Never once did you mention Vinu or Harsha in any of your calls or letters. Don't you think she felt it rather deeply?'

'I have changed a lot,' Gouramma said sadly. 'America has opened my eyes and I shall never make that mistake again. Will Vinu and Harsha never come back to this house? Can I not see Harsha ever?' Gouramma was now in tears.

Shamanna comforted his wife. 'Don't worry. There has been no fight. We can leave for Dharwad right now if you wish to see them and have a nice time together, provided you promise me one thing.'

'What is that?' Gouramma asked in surprise.

'You should not keep talking about America, its wealth and your Dollar Bahu.'

'Oh, don't worry, I won't,' she said. 'I won't, ever. I promise.'

With a deep sigh, she opened her purse to retrieve the keys to open her suitcase—and a hundred dollar bill fell out. It was the bill that Chandru had given her at the airport. But at that moment, it did not hold any charm, any power or any magic.

The invincible Dollar had fallen . . .

Sudha Murty